Beyond
the
Islands

Alicia Yanez Cossio

Translated by Amalia Gladhart

Printed in the United States of America

Library of Congress Control Number: 2001012345

Beyond the Islands

Alicia Yánez Cossío

Translator: Amalia Gladhart

ISBN 13: 978-1-60801-043-1

First Edition

Copyright © 2010 by UNO Press

PRESS

University of New Orleans Press
Managing Editor, Bill Lavender
http://unopress.org

Beyond
the
Islands

Alicia Yánez Cossío

Translated by Amalia Gladhart

Contents

Morgan

For some time now, Morgan had been feeling an unbearable itch at the base of the femur that, bereft of both tibia and fibula, still embraced tightly, if uselessly, a bit of almost immobile patella to which was joined a length of palo santo that was the extension of his lost left leg. His first wooden leg had been made of cedar. Many years ago, so many that it was impossible to recall the details, he had asked a carpenter to make him a leg out of cedar, thinking of cedar's incorruptibility, and the carpenter made it for him, but neither of them knew, nor could they know, that American cedars did not belong to the same family as the conifers with which Solomon built his temple, nor were they related to the Himalayan cedars, nor did they have anything to do with the symbol of long life in Biblical songs; this was a cedar with quite different properties.

And it happened that during one of the frequent eruptions that it was his lot to live through on the islands, Morgan was trapped between the rocks. Terrified, he watched the incandescent lava carry off a good chunk of his leg as if it were a straw. The wood's softness saved his life: he could crawl backwards and get himself to safety. Breathless and unipod, at the mercy of an infuriated Nature, he endured the onslaught of the hot waves until, without knowing how or when, he found himself lying on the shore while a rain of stones fell onto his body. He could only protect himself with his arms. He was corralled between the stones, unable to flee or to defend himself, as it must have happened to the woman taken in adultery of the Gospels and before that to the embracing couple of the Santa Elena Peninsula, their prehistoric burial so much older than the former. He watched the stones falling and he was unable to dodge; he saw them land and observed their size and thickness, and he heard the blows against his body even in the midst of the infernal din. The pain reached him from who knows where, and he could see his open flesh at the center of a stone's imprint and he felt an almost hot dampness as his blood slid agreeably over his skin like a caress. Furious and defenseless at the same time, he managed to take refuge in his own impotence only because he had nowhere else to hide.

When the rain of stones stopped, a small earthquake knocked them down again and he was freed from the tumulus, and then the sea made him a gift of a half-charred launch and he was able to climb aboard and set sail. But the launch ran the risk of disintegrating as it leaped, defenseless, over the waves of a sea that boiled like soup; the launch tipped from side to side, rising and falling with the waters that rose up like ramparts. Morgan bailed with his blistered, wounded hands, trying at the same time to maintain his grip on the sides of the boat. He tried every sort of pirouette and maneuver to keep his balance and not fall into the convulsing sea. And thus he continued for a long time: adrift, struggling tirelessly, under the iridescence of a crimson, apocalyptic sky that seemed to shudder and fall in pieces over the islands as from time to time the volcanic eruptions resumed. He felt, too, a volcano that erupted with stubbornness and rebellion within his own constricted chest, an eruption like an unfinished act of rebirth and death in a single moment. He struggled like Hemingway's old Santiago, the most solitary and tenacious protagonist in all of literature, conscious that a man like himself could be destroyed, but never vanquished.

Morgan hoped the launch might carry him to any one of the islands, but whenever he came close, the island would change shape in violent tremors. The air was thick and unbreathable; his lungs rejected its sulfur with an intermittent cough. Birds tried to spread their useless wings and fell back, choking and dispirited. Crazed fish crossed the surface of the water like arrows while others, lifeless, silvered the turbulent waters with their exposed undersides. The iguanas slithered inland and the tortoises cut themselves off from the islands, hiding their heads beneath their shells, which made the safest bunker.

Morgan, who did not know fear, was finally able to save himself. He knew that he had never struggled in vain. Crazed with thirst, bruised from head to foot and hungry, he arrived some days later, more dead than alive, at the same island of fire that had expelled him, and he began anew that solitary life of an ancient Robinson, an old sailor lamenting the loss of his cedar leg which he replaced with any old stick that might shore up his body while he gave himself over to the task of rebuilding his cabin, which could no longer remain in the same place, but had to be closer to the freshwater spring that had changed its location. He remade his hunting gear and his fishing tackle, and he felt again his solitude and the stormy love that would come to redeem him and that waited behind time's back.

Some years passed before Morgan was able to obtain his second leg, which he ordered from a cabinetmaker on the mainland. It was made of *guayacán*, the hardest, most incorruptible wood he could get, but it was so solid and heavy that it could never match the nervous activity of his body. His flesh seemed to repel the *guayacán*: bearing the same sign of durability, the two were unable to blend; like sticks and stones under the same roof, they couldn't get along, so that he finally put it in a corner once and for all and made his third leg all by himself. This was the one that had lasted the longest, although it was the most fragile, perhaps because it was made of native wood and Morgan, too, was endemic to the islands. While he felled and hewed the palo santo trunk, he seemed to hear a mysterious murmur that told him to be wary, that this third leg would play him false, but he paid no attention. He lacked the patience to accustom his body to the *guayacán*, and thus the unique qualities of the palo santo would bring about his death.

Morgan was older than all of the palo santo trees in the islands, older than all of the cedars and *guayacáns* of the mainland. The palo santo of his third false leg had achieved the perfect fusion with the scar tissue of his thigh and, trying to determine the cause of the tremendous itching, he began to detach it carefully, because he had never taken it off since he'd put it on, as if that were the most absolute condition of tolerance. When he had placed it to one side and peered in at the patella, he could just barely see a tiny black spot at the center; that was what generated the itching. It was in the middle of the purple scar, like macerated blood, sewn up by the crude method of stretching the skin to cover the flesh—an emergency seam, like the poor man's mending that stretches fabric to fool the cold; a rustic, charlatan's stitch, far from the stylistic refinements of plastic surgery, exactly the same as the hem that the settlers' wives used to close the sacks of salt that they shipped to the mainland.

The itch came from within, from the bone marrow, producing an unbearable irritation. Everything seemed to come from within, not from outside, because everything originated in his mind, which ordered and dominated his organism, consumed as it was by the ferocious battle to survive. His glands, his viscera, his hormones were all subject to his will: he was hungry, sleepy, or tired when he wanted to be. He was fully himself, enjoying the landscape of the islands, until the itch started up and made him sullen and ill-tempered.

As the itching became stronger, it stopped being an itch and became pain. His face, crossed and quartered by lines like the dry, eroded fields, was hardened, tanned by the sun and by the equatorial winds, and if it weren't for his light eyes and his European features, he would have looked like a black man, an angry, ill-natured black man who knew, better than anyone, the secret of the islands.

He had been crouched over the rough lumps of black lava for some time, taking the shade of a mangrove, hunkered down among the roots, while his pale eyes scrutinized the horizon, watching—his gaze tireless and fixed—the line that separated the sea from the sky and feeling, more strongly than at other times, the imperceptible line that existed between life and death, between being and non-being.

With one hand he scratched his sore thigh and with

the other he picked his teeth with a codfish bone. The sun hung belly down, reheating the basalt rocks; it was a gigantic, golden crab that absorbed the breeze and sucked the chlorophyll from the plants, leaving them withered and parched. The scaly marine iguanas, ordinarily black, now had the brilliant and variegated colors of the mating season which reminded him of the colors of Iridia's dresses. The bristling ridges of their backs resembled tridents, and from time to time they spat out excess salt, making a noise like the sound that turkeys make when they strut about like consecrated bishops. The iguanas were the miniature version of St. George's mythical dragon, newly expelled from the altars, and they, too, defended themselves against the force of the sun, changing position according to the hour of the day. Impassive and still, they raised their bulk, supporting themselves on their interminable tails and sharp extremities, and in this way avoided scorching themselves on the glowing rocks. Imperturbable and hieratic, they seemed to keep watch over Morgan's movements and to watch over the passage of time, stalled in the islands and stalled within Morgan's biology by the unheard-of obstinacy of his refusal to accept what is ordained for all mortals—namely, death—with whom he had been fighting a pitched battle since forever.

A heat like the dog days of summer rose slowly through his leg as if it had been pushed into the middle of a bonfire. The itching intensified. Suddenly, he spat out the codfish bone, which landed right at the foot of a wild cactus. He stood up and rubbed his hands against his threadbare trousers, which were coming apart at the seams, and began to cross the pointed black lava rocks by implausible leaps. It was a circus spectacle. His body, almost two meters tall, maintained an astonishing balance on the top of the cliff and it seemed impossible that there could be such synchronization of movement between an entirely worn-out canvas shoe on his right foot and a chunk of palo santo on the left, which neither slipped nor got caught in the fissures and which was so perfectly fused to his stump that he seemed to have been born with it. The wood had all the weaknesses and sensitivities of his aged flesh. It was an organic part of his body, integrated like any graft. The bark of the palo santo was the continuation of his hairy skin, and the wood seemed to have the arteries and the nerves of any flesh that might both hope and despair at the uncertain day of the final resurrection which, at bottom, didn't matter to him: he neither wanted it nor took it for a certainty, because the force of habitual doubt had allowed the reality that there was nothing, absolutely nothing, beyond the here and now to take root, and he had to struggle against nonexistence.

Out there on the line of the horizon, where no other inhabitant of the islands could distinguish anything, Morgan had managed to make out a dark point, no bigger than the head of a sardine: it was the *Floreana*.

The *Floreana* was coming from the mainland with its usual cargo of Kodaks, Pentax, and Canons swaying against the bellies of some fifty tourists who were going to see and to photograph the miracle of the prodigious islands, the ones that for many centuries were called the Enchanted Isles, because they had the property of appearing and disappearing in the middle of the sea, hundreds of miles from the mainland, so that they both were and were not before the eyes of the weary sailors who were unable to establish their true latitude. It was said that when the pirates headed deliberately for the islands to hide in their caves the fruits of their plunder, they didn't find them, but when they sailed toward other places, the islands appeared before them as though emerging from nothingness. For other sailors the islands, confused in the mist and in legend, were sometimes the Incas' Ninacumbi and Huachichumbi while at other times they were the Easter Islands, or the islands of Polynesia, always enigmatic and wonderful in the midst of the tempestuous sea and its far horizons. It was said that a general, one Villamil, made a voyage hauling the end of a cable that he pulled the length of the sea, sailing in a straight line, until he reached the islands and was able to tie them up and moor them firmly to the coast of the mainland where the other end of the cable was buried. Ever since they had remained in place, although now and again they returned to their enchantment of being and not being.

The tourists began to work their cameras, photographing the distant and elongated contours of the islands, and a few who knew their history worried that the islands would suddenly cease to be and would dissolve like a mirage, to the detriment of their curiosity and their pocketbooks. The cameras took shot after shot of the swift glide of the dolphins that guarded the boat, crossing fore and aft and playing at races, and of the sure flight of the gulls that barely skimmed the mantle of crystalline air and reflected, in their white feathers, the emerald color of the waters. The tourists spoke at the top of their voices in unknown languages; on deck, enthralled, they expressed the childish joy of good rich folk in exclamations of astonishment, while the ship approached the land that awaited them, inhospitable but seductive and mysterious.

Lost among the people crowded around the bow, insignificant and unrecognized, with her blue print dress that was like a uniform of poverty, without the ease of the tourists accustomed to traveling by sea and by air; without a camera; without English, German, or any other language besides that spoken among the sailors and the inhabitants of the islands, came Iridia with her bundle of clothes, her embossed leather coin purse clutched in her hand, and her freight of dreams that had jumped overboard and rode on the birds' wings to Morgan's arms, where they had taken refuge, making him tremble with a kind of love as stubborn as his struggle with death, one that was reborn, violent and incendiary, with the impassioned fury of the last chance. Iridia and Morgan had met on the mainland.

They looked at each other and immediately loved each other as if, across the centuries and the kilometers, there had existed two points, each seeking its vertex. He loved her fresh twenty years, her shyness like a restless dove's, her innocence overcome with tenderness, her transparent gaze. And she loved the fascination of his eyes, the rhythmic back and forth of his wooden leg; his words, that carried the flavor of a history book never written; the things that he knew and that seemed impossible to fit in a single brain, a compendium of a living, seafaring encyclopedia. She loved the experience of his long life and the way he fairly evaluated its characters and circumstances, as if they had been the ideas of a being who was returning from life after a long time. She never found another man like him, for her he was the only one, although the men of the islands lined up outside her door.

Morgan could be more than her father, her grandfather, even great-great-grandfather. In his shadow, she felt the security of the home that she had never had. She knew that he was old, but she saw how he overflowed with virility, even from his wooden leg, and she was fascinated when he told her that he had achieved longevity thanks to the liquor he distilled in his home still. Drop by drop, the invisible liquid finally emerged through a sieve comprised of one whole, fat chicken, a few steers' hooves, and a certain cactus that only he knew. Later he told her that the beverage was a substitute for the famous rum punch of his no less famous great-great-grandfather, Woodes Rogers.

Then Iridia saw in him more than an ordinary man, she saw him as a mythical being, like a demigod or a hero escaped from the neighborhood movie screen, and she knew that the wooden leg was not the result of the barracudas' teeth—as many people said—but that it was the result of far off endorsements signed when he was a pirate, an authentic pirate from the days when the Spanish galleons zigzagged across the seas trying to escape the greed of the immodest Virgin Queen. The dates didn't matter. Iridia was convinced that the era of Elizabeth and her corsairs coincided, no less, with the era of Eloy Alfaro, of which she had a fuzzy understanding because the old grandfathers would tell and retell their deeds and stories on holidays at sunset, before they went into the taverns.

Morgan had told her that she would be his third and last wife, when in fact she was the seventh. The others had died of the tedium, old age, and hard work that made up the common ailments of the islands. The pure sea air took it upon itself to push all sickness toward the mainland. Morgan hid the fact that he had been a pirate—only Iridia, who could understand so many things, knew—and the reason he hid was that he was afraid he might say more than he should and reveal the matter of the treasure. He smiled sarcastically and enigmatically when anyone mentioned the pirates' caves. His eyes flashed irony when he saw other foreigners like himself disembarking, equipped with modern apparatus and brand new radar with which they went from one spot to another looking for the treasure's lair. Only he knew its location. At times, when he had a few too many of his usual drinks, he spoke in a strange language, or told such unbelievable tales that the islanders crossed themselves upon hearing them, or celebrated them with high guffaws, as if they were flawed stories, poorly made. When they spoke to him, they called him *mister* with a certain respect that was not without irony, but behind his back they called him *tock-tock* after the persistent sound of his wooden leg which announced his presence and drew the longest of shadows across the sand.

No one in the islands ever guessed that he was the owner of the treasure that had carried so many expeditions to their ruin over so many years. In fact, Morgan did not really own the treasure. It had simply ceased to matter to him and he had forgotten its existence. He had lived his solitary life waiting, without knowing it, for a tumultuous love like the one he now felt for Iridia, one that would give meaning to his near-immortality because without it, what other meaning could his life, or his struggle with death, have had? He could not resign himself to the evidence; death represented for him absolute meaninglessness, the most complete outrage, the most grotesque philosophy.

The sight of the *Floreana* coming closer, riding the waves like a tired seal, made him forget the terrible itching. He watched the operation of dropping anchor and launching the boats, trying to discover among the silhouettes of the passengers the bride of his dreams with her long, silky hair, with her passion, her sweetness, her candor close to the surface. The tourists moved slowly, one by one, into the small launch that would carry them to shore. Time passed: the tourists had to disembark first, then the settlers with their pots and pans, and only afterward Iridia with her shyness.

Morgan grew tired of waiting and lay back down under the mangrove without missing a detail of the operation. He felt the itching more intensely than before and along with it a pain that traveled slowly over his body. Impatient, he began to beat on his wooden leg, syncopated blows with the edge of his hand. He stopped short, then went back to beating the peg at the spot corresponding to what should once have been an ankle and was no longer... His blood froze before the evidence. It was as if everything had collapsed in an instant, as if he had received a clubbing, a shove into the void, an internal rent harder and more violent than death itself, the idea of which he was unable to tame. The truth appeared to him thus, head on; he couldn't look at it from any other angle. There it was. There was neither doubt nor misunderstanding. It was before his eyes, immaculately naked and at the same time frankly bony, like all fundamental truths: the wood was hollow—hollow! He knew what that meant.

He stopped watching the *Floreana* and began to sweat copiously. Cold perspiration ran down his face, the drops caught in his lashes and trembled before they fell from the tip of his nose to the ground as if leaping off the springboard of death. His soaked shirt stuck to his body and the print took on the proportions of carnivorous flowers. Morgan dried the sweat and remained immobile in the face of fear. Not even when he had known that he had stronger and more bloodthirsty enemies eager to undertake a boarding action and annihilate his ship, nor when his ship caught fire on the high seas, nor when his injured foot became gangrenous and half his leg had to be cut off, nor when he was shipwrecked and found himself facing two enormous barracudas, nor in the din of the most ferocious combat, nor in the eruptions and earthquakes caused by the two thousand volcanoes of the islands, never had he felt what he felt now. It was the premonition that his efforts were good for nothing, that his ongoing struggle was the great defeat, and for the first time he experienced fear and he felt it traveling along the rails of his nervous system to alter his brain which had already become paralyzed.

The evidence of destruction was undeniable, and it was hard to admit that in the moment of the greatest hope of his life, when he awaited the dreamed-of bride, when his long days of waiting took on a purpose, his palo santo leg, mainstay of his aged body and companion in his travels was, in spite of sporadic sprinklings with kerosene and camphor, worm-eaten. A woodworm had gotten in through the base of the stick, right at the center, and on its voyage north it had run into the partial patella and had penetrated it until it reached the femur and with the worm had come the woodworm of death, which was eating away at his heart that was no longer young and his brain which was already worn out and the fingers of his hands that were beginning to feel the first symptoms of arthritis and the right leg which had begun to be jealous of the left and insisted on dragging. It was too late for Morgan.

He understood at once the significance of the itch and of the pain moving by millimeters through his body. A woodworm with wings, only one of the twelve classes of moths that existed in the islands, had contrived to make a nest in his wooden leg, hollowing it out from the inside and eating, gluttonously and without mercy, mouthfuls of the flesh invulnerable to time and bits of the bones older than all of the cedars, *guayacáns*, and palo santo trees of the island.

The paradox clobbered him, it wounded his heart and caught him full force with both hands in a bloodthirsty squeeze. He had overcome time, labors, hardships, dangers. He had achieved the most extraordinary longevity, and a simple, defenseless, miniscule worm was beginning to erode his Herculean form, because once the femur and its head were hollowed out, it would take the broad plain of the ilium, then the path of the coccyx and the sacrum, it would ascend the lumbar and dorsal vertebrae, it would stretch out across the clavicles, it would have a picnic on the scapulas, it would continue along the humerus, the ulna, the radius, the phalanges, it would travel slowly through the cervical vertebrae in order to have a rest in the brain, and then it would descend through the vertebral canal, destroying on its way the sternum and the framework of the ribs so as to continue with its devastating hurry until it reached the bones of the right side where perhaps it would take its last rest in the patella, it would make the last round trip through the tibia and the fibula, it would pause to freshen up in the cuboids and then conclude its trajectory in the metatarsals, from which it would prepare to emerge victorious, although terribly tired, through the big toe of the right foot, completing its life cycle and making an end to the overthrow of a whole human organism, eager and persevering in its right to flee destruction and nothingness and the unknown that it had never encountered.

Then it would not take long for Morgan to be reduced to a miniscule little pile of sawdust that would be swept away by the island wind. He went on beating on the leg with an inward and persistent fury, born of the evidence that no human being could achieve immortality. Sooner or later he would have to pay the tribute due for having seen the sun rise, for sitting down to watch the sunset, for breathing in the perfume of the flowers and the scent of the earth, for caressing a child, for feeling any form of love. Heavy tears of rage and helplessness rolled down the leathery skin of his face and his broad thorax seemed ready to burst with sorrow. He saw death, which he had tried to elude for so many years. He saw her approach, riding on the air. He had fought against the inevitability of death's dominion and he had even come to believe that he had beaten death, and when he was about to declare himself the absolute champion, the only one, the omnipotent, reality took up residence and with a simple gesture flipped the coin again, allowing the most miserable of insects, a simple woodworm, to bring down his crazy dreams of continuing to live and to love eternally. The lover of life and the former victor over death cried as he had never cried before. Sick with the fear of death, he howled in desperation, chewing his sorrow, coiling and uncoiling his sadness, writhing like a sculpture of Laocoön, trying to strangle the presence of the rotten, traitorous, and inclement death that had enveloped him in her knots and her nets. He was going to lose the fight and wind up exhausted.

It was low tide and the *Floreana* anchored far out. The boats finished ferrying the passengers to a small natural pier embedded in the reefs like a welcoming embrace. Iridia arrived at last, lost amidst the tourists' luggage, and the two lovers lost themselves in a long and tight, damp and shuddering embrace, because Morgan was still sobbing uncontrollably, his tears wiping out his lineage, the direct line of his genealogy, that of the legendary Woodes Rogers who in 1709, following a crude and violent attack, sacked and burned Guayaquil, making the city tremble with horror, and who later dedicated himself to sowing terror on the seas, seizing any galleon that came within reach, and thus it was that he managed to capture the *Sol de Oro*. When his fearsome pirates threw themselves into the fray and boarded her, they found in the depths of her dark hold an immense golden chain marvelously worked by the Incas. Seeing it, Woodes Rogers threw himself upon it, killed all of the crewmen in cold blood, ferried the chain to his ship, and sank the *Sol de Oro*, which would never reach its destination. But his ship could not keep afloat with the weight of the stolen chain in addition to the weight of consciences hardened by crime, so that sailing became slow and difficult, preventing him from reaching Europe. He had no other alternative than to quietly approach the islands and hide his booty in their depths.

Morgan inherited from his great-great-grandfather the secret of where the chain was buried and the secret of long life. Woodes Rogers was already devoted to the fear of death that he would hand down to Morgan. After burying the chain, his crew began to disappear, decimated by yellow fever, but he remained invulnerable, unable to leave the site of the treasure. His ship was a mobile hospital where death tried to hunt him down and he, eluding death, never stopped giving orders and cursing, inspecting the ship from stem to stern, smoking like a chimney with a fat cigar hanging from his lips and drinking constantly, to stave off the germs, the rum punch that could topple any other pirate.

Every day he counted the men that remained and replaced the moribund with the ailing. The leeches were unable to meet the demand, swollen as they were with so much virulent blood, and he added and subtracted the members of his impoverished and squalid crew, cursing his luck, while the ship turned full around every afternoon to bury in the deep waters another body that went to the bottom carrying with it the secret of the treasure. He fought death face-to-face, and it was said that he spent years traveling from Guayaquil to Liverpool in search of a new crew that would be loyal to him and wouldn't mutiny once they were in possession of the chain, but he never managed to complete the full number of crewmen before his footprints, his ambitions, and his curses were ultimately lost and he was never heard from again. He must have died in some port without having been able to put the chain to sea. Not even Morgan had further details. He knew the place where it was buried because he had always known it. The chain was there, for him, and he had even stroked each of its links with his hands. It remained buried at the foot of one of the islands' two thousand volcanoes.

It seemed that the chain might have trapped him, preventing him from leaving for other places, but the islands were the ideal place in which to elude death and although death knew where he was and what he was doing, Morgan could defend himself against her spying by eating, daily, one of the seven types of tortoise meat that had the power to preserve life. Death had granted him a long respite, but that was coming to an end and Morgan knew it.

Morgan took a long time to comprehend that the defiance of death was every bit as important as his reason for living, but he needed love to give himself strength and so he almost forgot about the existence of the enormous chain. He knew with absolute certainty that wealth could not make mortals happy, and that many men had died violent deaths because of it, passing through a painful transition from their familiar state to nothingness. He knew that, for wealth, men had become degenerate and degraded, he knew that gold bore the most harmful of influences because it had the power to drive mortals crazy. It wasn't worth it to revive dormant or latent ambitions by digging up the treasure. The terrible buccaneers would reappear with deadlier weapons, piracy would reestablish itself with new corsairs, it would be difficult to predict what catastrophes and of what severity a buried treasure of that size would occasion. The chain should remain coiled upon itself, like an ancient serpent forever sleeping through the winter of the centuries.

Morgan was beside himself in the face of his imminent death. For one instant, he even thought of using the chain to achieve a kind of hibernation, but he quickly felt tired and realized that he no longer knew if he wanted life or not, and life began to cause him pain. He ached at being on earth. The dawns and the nightfalls of the centuries began to pain him. His having been born began to pain him, and yet he needed to live for Iridia, and he rebelled against the death which was already installed in his ancient bones and made itself felt with each step. He even came to hear the sound of the macabre one. The bones of the bony one clattered against his own bones, which were already becoming the woodworm's sawdust.

More than the pain of his bones, what hurt him was Iridia's presence, and then he thought he might, just once, make use of the treasure, a small part of it, just one link of the chain. He wanted a piece for Iridia, whose sole property comprised a bundle of clothes, a nearly empty coin purse, and a newly-minted youth. And also, at the last minute, he began to think of his children: how many were there? He didn't know, nor was it possible to count them. Many would have died years ago. Others would have moved to the mainland. They must be scattered here and there in various adventures and different trades. But it would be easy to identify them because of the unmistakable color of their eyes, the feline and iridescent color set in a clear and penetrating gaze that was like a birthmark that they would never lose, nor would they be able to lose it in succeeding generations. But, thinking better of it, he decided to forget about them; he could not know what use they might make of the treasure although, buried within his pain, another class of unfamiliar pains began to come to him.

So after welcoming Iridia and telling her passionately how much he loved her, he settled her as best he could in his old wood hut, the residue of the great crates in which a whole arsenal, both destructive and defensive—in truth, they amounted to the same thing—had arrived during the Second World War, when the islands were the clandestine theater of every international intrigue.

Iridia, worn out by the emotions of the encounter and the hardships of the long journey, fell sound asleep. Then Morgan took a jug of water, a little food, and his inseparable bottle of booze, gave a kiss to Iridia's dreams as she smiled at him from the dream world's great beyond, and without further delay, he began to walk. At the midpoint of the path, he detoured a ways to reach the home of San Pío Pascual and Santa Livina. He was going to make a long journey, but the physical condition of his legs was not what it had been, and it was quite possible that he would never return. He left the path moved by a premonition. He carried the anxiety of having called Iridia to share with him affection and protection; he could not leave her alone and abandoned among the black ridges of lava and the lust of men as hungry for young women as the islanders were.

He had known about masculine lust ever since he'd seen the ships that anchored in the islands and saw how, without even waiting for a launch to carry them to shore, the crew would throw themselves headfirst into the sea amidst savage howls and how they swam after the female seals so as to copulate indiscriminately with them, while the pod's desperate male pursued one female and then another before she died, because for the barbarous joining each had been mortally beaten to enjoy the orgasm of death. At times he, too, had mixed promiscuously with the astonished seals, because in so many years of existence there was no human or inhuman act that he had not experienced. That was when Morgan cursed his fate as a poor mortal and remembered the treasure, and when macabre images of his existence, and the innocent recollections of his distant childhood, paraded before his eyes, and he drank himself unconscious.

In all the years San Pío Pascual and Morgan had lived in the islands, they never once exchanged even half a word; Morgan was repulsed by the very presence of Santa

Livina, San Pío Pascual's nasty shadow, and all the efforts of the priest with his shepherd's spirit in search of lost sheep, shattered against the cold indifference of the pirate. That day, when San Pío Pascual saw Morgan approaching his house, walking with an unusually feeble rhythm, he jumped to his feet and his breviary crashed into the small heap of corn that the chickens were pecking. Constrained by surprise, San Pío Pascual waited for him to come closer. Morgan had resolved to go and make confession to him, not so as to beg for absolution—for he repented of nothing—but rather to share the secret of the treasure under the protection of a seal, which was perfectly admissible in a man who had killed in the name of religion and who before throwing himself into a boarding action, had crossed himself, holding his cutlass between his teeth, as if the act were a good luck ritual, and who had prayed for good aim before firing his cannons against defenseless ships. He had lived during an era in which religion was a question of politics, in which pirates and corsairs were subtly distinguished, and the rites were incorporated into custom.

When Morgan was close to San Pío Pascual, he broke the silence of the afternoon that was beginning to shake off its drowsiness with an abrupt, "Good afternoon, *Mosén*."

"Good afternoon, but I am not called *Mosén*, my name is San Pío Pasual," responded the worthy of the islands, tucking his cassock between his legs—a very difficult operation because at that moment the breeze blew stronger, swelling the insides of his long black gown, black as the intentions of Santa Livina, who left hanging in the air her supposed witch's broom. (The broom suited her, and even seemed to boast a brake and clutch with which she could fling herself into a crazy nocturnal race through the air.) Santa Livina stopped sweeping up the scattered corn and leaned on her broom in expectation of what might come to pass between the two men who had never before greeted one another. When the wind abated and San Pío Pascual accomplished what he was trying to do with his cassock, he invited Morgan to have a seat under the trellis of bougainvillea that offered a protective shade, and he extended his hand, trying to erase with that gesture any difference that might have existed between the two men, who after all were the most important men in the islands, given that the officers of the military garrisons had arrived only recently and the civil authorities, the few foreigners, and the merchants were situated at the level of outsiders and social climbers, the same as the tourists who came and went without anyone giving them any importance.

"Good morning, Your Holiness," Morgan responded hesitantly, sitting down in the chair he was offered and trying to remember the magic word with which he could convey the purpose of his visit without appearing to lessen his manliness. But he had either forgotten the magic word that would unravel the tangle of his feelings at the precise moment when death was approaching, or else it didn't exist. He couldn't say exactly what he wanted because the matter was too hard to pin down and words became elusive, and above all common sense got in his way as if it were an inopportune witness, as unwelcome as the presence of Santa Livina who went on sweeping the corn, kernel by kernel, besieged by the insatiable hens. The two were standing before an act that was too intimate and they could not come to the point.

"Good father..." he went on, without finding the one word that would make the other man understand that he had made the journey to his home in order to recognize a spiritual authority beneath which he needed to place himself, where he could take shelter for a moment, just a moment, so as to say what he needed to say, in the shade of the rosy bougainvillea that dropped its petals in the wind.

"Well, Morgan, I am at your service."

"It's that... not being accustomed..." He tried to make excuses and to follow the path the other man had opened, but he remained at a standstill and at that moment Santa Livina appeared on the pretext of a pitcher of lemonade, trying to get closer and ingratiate herself so as to be able to discover for herself the reason for this unexpected visit. But Morgan broke off abruptly with a grimace that did not go unnoticed by San Pío Pascual. He scratched his sore leg and shifted in the folding chair that creaked under his weight, at the same time that he heard a strange creak within his body, a sound that was none other than the creaking of his bones.

"By hell!" he muttered through his teeth, remembering that he ought to be giving his wooden leg the consideration due an ailing limb.

San Pío Pascual was startled by the bit about hell, and Santa Livina stood up, offended, and left without serving the lemonade. The atmosphere cleared, and San Pío Pascual once again took up his tolerance, asking Morgan about the reason for his visit and telling him, so as to facilitate the dialogue, that he might think of him as if he were a friend.

"That is what I do *not* want," Morgan responded, preparing himself nonetheless for a friendly confidence, because it would be impossible to proceed otherwise.

San Pío Pascual again presented himself as a fully consecrated person, all charity and good intentions. Even without words, the wall of isolation that he had maintained through the years began to crumble softly, until Morgan dropped on the ground, as if it were a heavy load of firewood, the reason for his unwonted visit: "I want to use that seal, or whatever the devil it's called," he said once and for all.

"Confession? You want to make confession?" asked San Pío Pascual, completely surprised, unable to convince himself that he had before him a coreligionist asking for his services—knowing, in spite of everything, that Morgan was an old drunkard who even had a home still for his private use; that he was probably even an atheist, given the way he blasphemed; knowing him as a habitual sinner of whom it was said that nearly all of the islands' inhabitants were his offspring. But Morgan remained seated in a respectful pose, in view of which San Pío Pascual took off his shabby straw hat, made the sign of the cross, turned away from the other's steely eyes, bowed his head and, lacing the fingers of his pudgy hands, prepared himself to receive a broadside of sins: "*O tempora, o mores.*"

Santa Livina, who had been observing them from a distance, returned quickly and made as if to serve the lemonade. Morgan rejected it, in spite of his thirst, so as to owe her no gratitude whatsoever, and when San Pío Pascual told her no, that he was hearing confession, Santa Livina was so amazed at what she heard, that she spilled the lemonade, splashing them both. Begging their pardon, she went away to prepare one that wouldn't be so sour, even though they were scraping the bottom of the sugar sack.

Then Morgan told him his whole life from beginning to end, without leaving out the fact that at one time he was a pirate, direct descendent of Woodes Rogers, along with all the rest of it. San Pío Pascual listened beatifically, as one who listens to an interesting legend about the islands, but he couldn't swallow the pirate bit, so he reminded Morgan kindly that they weren't just chatting or telling stories, they were engaged in the sacrament of confession, and even though they were at that moment under the shade of the rosy bougainvillea and not inside a confessional and within the church that had not yet been built—due to the laziness of the islanders—they were observing a ritual that demanded the utmost respect, devotion, and piety. A little resentful, he once again wrung his pudgy hands, repeating his refrain: "*O tempora, o mores.*"

"If you don't believe the part about being a pirate, I'll say I was a corsair…"

"Come, Morgan, don't exaggerate."

Then the old pirate drew from the depths of his pocket a small, four hundred year old coin that he carried like a talisman. San Pío Pascual knew nothing of numismatics, but he knew a little something of history, enough to put two and two together, and he was finally convinced of everything Morgan told him, with exact dates, about the capture of the *Sol de Oro* by his great-great-grandfather. Without going into detail and without revealing the spot where the chain was buried, he described how it was so big, so solid and well-wrought, that it took more than twenty men to move it.

Santa Livina came back with another pitcher of lemonade. This time they did drink, in silence, because it was necessary to take a break in the sacrament, and also because she took them by surprise. When the glasses were empty, they thanked her, and then San Pío Pascual tried to get rid of her by sending her to prepare two cups of coffee, which was the first thing that occurred to him.

When Santa Livina left, Morgan told him the story of his three wooden legs, and of how the current one was worm-eaten and how he felt the tenacious and constant work of the woodworm's growing body. He told him that his days were numbered and he spoke of the anxiety he felt because Iridia would be left alone and abandoned in the islands; he spoke of how, although he had earlier decided against it, now he thought that perhaps, yes, he did have a feeling of responsibility or something similar toward the hundreds of children scattered throughout the islands and on the mainland. "Because all of them, everyone around here, young and old, are my children."

And he sat for a long time thinking that it no longer mattered that he maintain his strength of character and that if he was waffling between yes and no, doubting at every instant, it was because his time was short and the doubt made him more human and less an animal.

San Pío Pascual followed the thread of Morgan's thoughts with difficulty. "Who are your children?"

"All of those who have green eyes," Morgan continued, fixing his eyes on the startled eyes of San Pío Pascual, as if to say to him: look, look well at the color of my eyes. And he told him that he was thinking he ought to divide the treasure between Iridia and all of his offspring. San Pío Pascual opened his eyes wide and reminded him like a good Christian of the poor, of the widows and orphans, and Santa Livina came back at just that moment with the two cups of coffee. San Pío Pascual told her irritably that she should wait a while, that he had not yet finished administering the sacrament.

Morgan responded that perhaps, that if there was time, he would take this advice into account, and he finally exacted a promise, under oath, that if he died before the appointed time, San Pío Pascual would be responsible for sharing out justly and equitably a portion of the treasure.

"Do you swear?"

"That is not necessary," San Pío Pascual responded. "We are under the seal of a sacrament; moreover, do not forget that I am a priest."

Morgan answered that he knew that, and for that very reason needed him to swear like a man. San Pío Pascual jumped. He didn't know whether to get angry or not. He had heard about Morgan's violent temper. He thought it over, rubbing his pudgy hands. It would be neither worthwhile nor prudent to argue with him; not every penitent was the owner of a treasure.

"Very well. I swear as a man that I will do it."

"Good. Then have a drink," said Morgan, uncorking his bottle.

"Morgan, you are making confession!" shouted San Pío Pascual, deeply offended.

"Just in case," responded the other man, fixing his feline eyes upon him, which amounted to a command. San Pío Pascual, daunted, grabbed the bottle and took a drink. The liquid burnt his chaste larynx, path of Hail Marys and related expressions, as if it were a burst of flame.

"By Satan, you're a good man!" Morgan replied, laughing with a trace of sadness when he saw the other's flushed face and the eyes that seemed ready to run right out of their sockets after a gulp of fresh water. Then Santa Livina, who had not missed a bit of the spectacle, ran back with the coffee tray hoping to discover what strange turn the sacrament was taking, but San Pío Pascual found the coffee watery and told her so. Grudgingly, the woman went to make it stronger, casting him as she went a terrifying look: you will tell me about it when the visitor leaves.

In the midsummer heat, the two dissimilar and distant men downed another drink to seal their pact. Morgan was satisfied, while San Pío Pascual fanned himself with his hands and opened his mouth disproportionately wide to drink in the wind of the quiet afternoon. Before Santa Livina could return, the two men said goodbye with a firm handshake. Only when Morgan turned his back and began to move away, placing his ailing foot gently, did San Pío Pascual remember to absolve him and bless him like any son of God. He was left absorbed and confused by the secret, he almost felt upon his own poor shoulders the weight of the entire chain. How long could the commitment of the seal of the confessional endure? How long with Santa Livina at his side? She had returned with the coffee, good and strong, and on seeing that Morgan was no longer there, she grew choppy as the waves and poured it angrily onto the thirsty ground.

It was just as well that Morgan had refused to reveal where the treasure was buried, but when he did come back, they would have a more detailed conversation, a conversation between men, outside the compromising sacrament. They had become friends, he had liked the pirate in spite of the liquor. He began to distribute the treasure in his mind. Santa Livina didn't take her eyes off him. Standing in front of him, with her hands on her hips, like the handles of an old and battered coffee pot, imperceptibly tapping her foot, she waited for him to share with her the reason for the unexpected visit. She was consumed with impatience. She couldn't stand how he kept pushing her to one side, while he, without taking notice of anything else, was working it all out: a little to begin the construction of the church because it was high time to start to raise it. Another bit to build the parish house because this here was a piece of shit. Another bit to found a Catholic school, with nuns, because Miss Estenia's one-room Genoveva de Brabante School was secular and co-educational and wasn't good for anything. Another bit to get that Santa Livina off his back, who acted like his mother, though she wasn't, and who pierced his brain with her inquisitorial looks. It would be easy to find a man who would want to marry a rich woman but... Could there be a husband for Santa Livina? Another bit for his five nieces who, besides being ugly, couldn't find husbands. And for So-and-So and What's-His-Name and that other fellow who had those light eyes and must be direct descendents. And finally for this Iridia who he didn't even recognize because she had only disembarked that morning. And he couldn't forget the tithes and first fruits now that he had been named executor and there was enough for everyone. San Pío Pascual extended the list beyond the islands and the mainland, he had passed through the Holy Land and was arriving in Rome, the cradle of Christianity, when Santa Livina, unable to bear it any longer, slapped him. San Pío Pascual turned on her not because of the personal offense but because of the sacrilege and Santa Livina, conscious of what she had done, knelt at his feet so that he might absolve her.

Morgan had been walking some three kilometers over the sharp-pointed lava rocks. The heat was infernal. He was thinking that he should only pull off five or six links of the chain. That would be sufficient. Or perhaps the best thing would be to remove just one for Iridia and no one else. It was hard to decide. He was tired and sore. He walked through a desolate land sparsely dotted with occasional cacti that gave no shade, but only the appearance of a very peculiar desert. The cacti had evolved until they had changed shape. They had learned to defend themselves against the voraciousness of predators by making their fleshy leaves grow above very tall trunks. Morgan knew the way perfectly, he was just about to reach the shade. Several times he turned his head for a peek to make certain that Santa Livina wasn't following him. He had barely arrived at the midpoint of the journey when suddenly everything, absolutely everything, came to an end: Crack! His wooden leg broke into two pieces.

He was far from any human contact, unable to either advance or retreat, carrying with him the necessary liquid for a round-trip journey and in a place that amounted to marking the trail. When San Pío Pascual noticed he was so many days late in appearing and went to look for him—if he could guess the direction he had taken—he might find him already reduced to ashes by the burning sun. When Iridia, surprised by his absence, went out in search of him, he would already be dead. No one in the islands must know the direction he had taken, so he dragged himself a few meters to throw them off track. When he could do no more, he sat down to wait. He felt how the woodworm traveled rapidly through his bones. It must already be letting itself fall through the canal of the tibia. Its rush was greater and more urgent than was Morgan's struggle. It had to complete its circuit around his aged skeleton. Nothing could check that destructive march because Morgan had fallen. Half the distance still remained to be covered in order to reach the site of the treasure. Just a few meters back he had left the zone close to the sea; he had fallen in the zone of the thorny scrub land, humid and stifling, where the scarce trees covered with lichen gave the appearance of sinister ghosts. A terrible place in which to die and cease to be. After a time, a bit of shade reached him, although it was unnecessary because the sun was sinking into the sea. He understood that only a few moments of life remained to him, he swallowed the liquor that he had and he buried himself deep in thought. He tried not to allow himself to be beaten by desperation.

The bony one was spying on him from behind the stunted thickets. She had been following him since he left the home of San Pío Pasucal and Santa Livina. The toothless one was there and for nothing in this world did he want to make her happy with his weakness and his frailty. He should receive her face to face, with the defiant courage he had had all his life, so as to show her how men die. To encourage himself at the moment of truth, he grabbed hold with all his strength—the last strength he had—of the image of Iridia, the being he had most loved in all his long existence. Thus, when the enemy finally touched him, she would be unable to see the terror in his green eyes, but rather the sparkle of a lover's eyes which must have a brilliance that would be unfamiliar to the hangwoman, the one who grants no pardon, the real one.

At daybreak, when Brigita's roosters began to sing, Iridia startled awake and heard the stentorian voice of Morgan calling her. She leapt up and began to run. Without having ever been in those solitary regions, she passed through all of the places where Morgan had been a few hours earlier. She went directly, without hesitation, as if she were an arrow that was certain of its target, and when the sun began to rise, she arrived at Morgan's inert body. She saw his wooden leg broken in two pieces. She saw him stretched out face up and it seemed to her that he still smiled at her from the certain and infinite great beyond, and she was left mute with surprise when she saw that his canvas shoe was moving, and that from one of its many holes was beginning to emerge, dragging itself, a sticky larva, and when the larva came in contact with the morning air, it shuddered and out burst a pair of transparent wings, like cellophane, with which it began to flutter around the body toppled by death. When the first of the sun's rays touched Morgan's outstretched body, the butterfly stopped flying. It stood upon the sunbeam and, as if it were a mechanical escalator, without even fluttering its wings or moving at all, it climbed up the light along a straight line toward the center of the sun.

Iridia cried out and threw herself on Morgan's body, but her head hit the ground. Morgan's body was hollow inside! It was the shadow of a ghost. And then the wind began to carry off the old, worn clothing in a whirlwind of ashes, and of all that body, so beloved and so sturdy, all that remained was a little pile of dust that Iridia hurried to gather and collect in her hand so as to take it with her, in open quarrel with the wind that tried to take it away.

She retraced her steps, clasping to a chest heaving with sobs all that remained of Morgan. She returned to the town, and when she told what had happened, she was more surprised still when no one gave any importance to what she said. No one save Brigita, who drew her to her bosom, caressed her head and took her to her own home, where she prepared for her the infusion of the seven spirits that she knew how to make and that made everyone feel better.

It was as if Morgan had been outside reality, as if he had never existed or had died centuries before. Still, people wanted to know why Iridia cried so disconsolately and they wanted to see what she held in her fist. They wanted to see with their own eyes what it was that she kissed and guarded so passionately in her hand.

Alirio

oetry gushed out of him. Alirio was a poet and he wrote his poems without rest or measure. His hand was numb and stiff from so much writing, and he even tried to tame his left hand so as to make himself ambidextrous. Poems came out through the pores of his skin with the same biological ease as when he perspired under the sun. His inspiration was rich and vital like the jungle vegetation that overruns every parameter of possibility: clothes hung on a wire to dry became an alexandrine sonnet. A scrap of paper tossed about on the wind became a ballad in the classic meter. At night, when he stretched out on his narrow cot and tried to recover his energies, as he took off his shoes, a hole in his sock would inspire a lyric and then he would not rest after all; he would not recover his energies but would remain awake and shoeless, struggling until dawn with the problem of assonance. A miserable *café con leche* inspired an ode in lines of five syllables, and when he left his room to breathe a little sun, a woman dressed in black passing on the street would be transformed into an elegy. He wrote unrestrainedly, immoderately, without schedule or calendar, as if he had been born for this reason alone and as if the haste to say everything that he had inside him was due to the fact that death was nipping at his heels.

Alirio looked fat, but he wasn't. He was as thin as any poet who lives off his poetry and with his poems. Yet in spite of his Becquer-like pallor, he looked well-nourished, even with the circles under his perpetually wakeful eyes and his premeditated solitude as he fled the company of men. His deep and sunken eyes sought to go inward, to pass through his entire being and look himself in the brain, so as to capture the precise psychic mechanism of the equation that he had discovered, namely: metaphor is equal to poetry as poetry is equal to truth. He wanted to see the mental duality of the image vs. the word. He longed to see the stereotype of the idea, the metaphysical process of the transference that gave to one thing the name of another; he wanted to verify, enraptured, how a synecdoche or a metonymy might appear out of elements that at first glance seemed accidental and yet were not. He was dying to see the genesis of the symbol as it found its place among slant rhymes and full rhymes and he tried to look inside himself in order to draw this feeling out, to launch it on the words that at times escaped him or became entirely lost in his desperate, subjective diving, while his scant energy, his great spiritual and intellectual reserves, were left waiting in the long and solitary struggle. When he managed to capture the words, it was like waking from a dream.

He looked fat because all of the pockets of his never-new suit were filled with papers: in his trouser pockets, at the outer edges of his body, were the blank sheets, ready for when he might need them, anxious to be filled with lines of fine, closely-spaced letters. His jacket pockets held the rough drafts and the notes in which a weak, virgin, newborn inspiration still trembled, almost without form, not yet wrapped in the proper word; trembling and kicking like a tiny worm stretched out on a cabbage leaf, without a suitable dress in which to show itself to the curiosity or rapture, and, who knows, perhaps to the repudiation— because he had to be prepared for anything—perhaps to the incomprehension and even the ridicule of an insipid and vulgar public. All of his other pockets were filled with sheets ordered and classified by themes that went alphabetically from the A of amour, allegory, anxiety, etc., to the Z of Zen, zodiac and Zarathustra, and that contained, fresh and raw, the first impressions that later, in the solitude of his horribly disordered and yet private room, by force of patience and hard work, he would manage to make into emotions with a suitable form and to then move, later, to his inner breast pockets. Where other men kept their billfolds, close to the heat wrung from the heart, he kept the definitive poems eager to cross the threshold of the press and find their place on the dais of fame and then, yes, permit the Parca to approach with her toothless grin, with her harsh scythe and her black rags.

From behind he looked fat, though he had the nervous agility of a little bird on the lookout for seeds holding kernels of metaphor or small pits of trope. When he walked, it made one think of the swallow on crutches that César Dávila Andrade encountered when he spoke of Laura. If he had been close to a flame, he would have caught fire as completely and quickly as a doll made of tinder, volatilizing his spirituality of leathery skin and bones in the style of the long-suffering Knight of la Mancha.

He wrote as if at any moment death would say to him: let's go. When he was absorbed in his papers, he would stand up suddenly and for no reason, as if to breathe. He felt an intense flame that consumed and stung him from within, a real and tangible heat that could be registered with a Fahrenheit thermometer. It seemed as if his gray matter were dissolving, hampering his ability to analyze situations or recognize the ordinary things that fell outside the confines of the world of creation, where he alone could enter, giving himself the luxury of closing the door on those things that were the greatest concerns of other mortals. He lived entirely absorbed, from head to foot, with the single idea of continuing to write and finally finishing what he had to say before the arrival of the early-riser.

Every day, he emptied his pockets, looking over his papers and classifying them. The sheets of paper passed methodically from his trouser pockets to his jacket pockets and from there to his inside pockets. He crossed out, corrected, punctuated and in this daily and continuous operation his life slipped away like a trickle of water toward the ocean. The few calories he managed to wolf down when he recalled that he had other needs were of no use. He lived hunched over his table, shuffling papers, ruminating over assonances, materializing a sensibility that was as fine as a violin string, as a young pigeon's white feather, as a stylized ballerina, as Medardo Angel Silva's famous:

> *So airy, so fleeting, so divine*
> *we cannot know if she wants to fly or dance*
> *and her body turns to a delicate wing*
> *as if the breath of God sustained her stance.**

He was always short of time with which to set down in writing the innumerable sensations he experienced that became poems through the magic of words, lines that he polished from time to time with the patience of a haggard,

---

*From the poem *Danse D'Anitra.*

night-owl of a goldsmith in the heat of an inspiration that was like a congenital fever with lyrical chills.

He wrote and wrote, tireless and methodical, without wasting time on superfluous conversations, still less in Bohemian gatherings. He was not one of those poets who need alcohol or drugs to limber up his imagination or to activate his cerebral mechanism. He needed only pencil and paper to enter the pure essence of metaphor. He read little, not because he didn't enjoy it, but because his time fell short of his hurry and reading was a luxury he could not allow himself. He lived enclosed within the circle of a fearful and eternal solitude. He did not fight death like Morgan; he ran before her.

Alirio was born a poet and would die as one. From boyhood he had had the power to look at things from a secret angle and so discover their souls, grasp the message that all beings carried within and translate it into his own language, using the inexhaustible flow of his tenderness in the face of the overwhelming force of mediocrity, and he sometimes suffered a pain so great that it did not fit within his breast. His heart would beat faster when he was at the height of his creation, and the tachycardia was so long and so intense that his heart—which they say does not feel pain—truly hurt him with a stabbing pain, like an electrified organ, like the flesh that begins to suffer from abuse, like the pain of a muscle that begins to contract out of biological self-defense.

Ten years before, in the capital, over a table littered

with cups of coffee, empty bottles, and ashtrays filled with butts, a panel of poetry judges had given birth to him for the second time at the age of twenty some years and he made his debut as the winner of the first national prize. The next year he was declared the winner in the Golden Apple competition. Two years later he won the Silver Cherry. The following year he won another contest and this time it was international. From that point on, he became a dangerous player on the cultural scene: any contest he entered was a contest he won. He had managed to publish more than a dozen books that were well received by serious critics and roundly abused by the envious and resentful who said that it wasn't possible, that he neglected form, that he didn't develop his themes in any depth, that it was just pure words with no content, that he didn't toe the party line, that he repeated himself with each book, that he didn't pick and choose, that he wrote for an elite, that the message— if there was one—was incomprehensible, that he wasn't a poet but rather a machine for making facile and simplistic rhymes. The twelve books were nothing compared with the thousands of verses he still had in preparation and the millions of rhymes still in the process of gestation. Given the prodigious, almost rabbit-like fertility of his extraordinary poetic inspiration, he might well have been the sole, authentic rival of Lope de Vega.

But it happened that one morning, a gelid city morning— which was the last line he had written, but which he didn't really like, although he had already played his intellectual trick with the antithesis of bucolic, which was what he wanted to write about—he got stuck on the word "city," which didn't convince him, and... and... and... period. He could not go on. Once or twice he had experienced this kind of blockage, this kind of amnesia after such unwonted mental activity, and he went back over his other papers so as to finish the bit about bucolic later and he found that he was blank, dry, empty, without a drop of water, as if the intermittent spring of the poem had moved to his brain. It had run dry, without cause, without motive, suddenly, as when he woke in the morning from a bad dream or was left with the soap on his skin and shaving foam in his sparse beard because the landlady had turned off the water. He was stuck with the bitter taste in his mouth.

All day long, the papers that he carried in his outer pockets remained blank, and they remained so for days. Alirio remained immobile, stalled in his astonishment, like the hands of a clock stopped at twelve-thirty on a ghostly night. He was dry as a tangerine peel in the sun. Blank as the bleached ribs of a camel dead of thirst in the desert for thousands of years. Dazed, with his eyes open, looking at real, precise, concrete things, but without being able to discern even a shred of the soul that each one held. Stunned and gaping as if he had received a blow to the head and didn't know who he was.

Desperate, he put away the papers that were in his upper pockets, he put them together with the others, made a packet tied up with string, and like a person preparing his luggage for a journey to an unknown country, he left them on the table. Then he began the desperate search for his muse. He looked for her in his pockets, between the bed sheets, in the disorder of his writing desk, in the rays of the sun that seemed to him crooked, in the twinkle of the stars that seemed to flicker out forever, in the capricious shapes of the clouds that were ever more monotonous, in the hearts and the dresses of women who seemed to him mannequins, among men and their tedious efforts, in the innocence of children who seemed to him stupid. And he began to analyze everything with an icy logic, to examine himself, thinking that perhaps he needed a purgative or some vitamins, ferociously hurt at feeling this strange dryness, this horrible common sense, and he wanted to know exactly what had happened, whether he had lived too quickly and was starting to slide down the slope toward old age, if these were César Vallejo's "blows in life so powerful... I don't know," * if it was the solidification of the medulla of his brain, whether it was this or was that.

Alirio continued his search within black sorrow, within fleeting happiness, in the long nights of insomnia, in the instant pleasure of sex, in the interminable hours of vigil, and when he understood once and for all that there was no cure because his muse had abandoned him and was beyond his reach, he went out in pursuit of the ingrate and he looked for her on every street, in cities large and small, he climbed the high mountains, he went to the forest swarming with

* First line of Vallejo's *Los heraldos negros*. Trans. Clayton Eshelman.

insects and wild beasts, he walked the banks of the swiftly flowing rivers and beside the irrigation ditches rimmed with watercress. Without determining her whereabouts, he went to bars and taverns where others of his ilk tended to gather, he inspected them from head to foot and concluded that his muse could not hook up with any of them: his muse was slender and delicate, she hated alcohol, foul language, sex, and politics. Desperate, he was left not knowing what to do because the only thing he had done up until then was write line after line; he didn't know what course he might take nor where to go.

Leaning against a light post that barely cast a glow, smoking one cigarette after another and pondering his concentrated anguish, all of a sudden he heard a *tock-tock* that made his hair stand on end and loosened his bowels and his knees. He watched the approach of a corpulent shadow that seemed to engulf him while his racing heart echoed in the steps of the shadow's wooden leg. He saw the flash of a pair of light and terrible eyes and he remembered the sea. Though he had never heard of Morgan, Alirio knew it was he. When he recovered from the spectral vision, he was already planning another trip. He would go to the only place that was left: to the fabulous islands that everyone talked about and that very few had seen; it was almost certain that his muse might be found in those latitudes.

He organized the mobile archive of his papers and prepared for the crossing. Travel to the islands was expensive. He sold his bed, his table, his typewriter, his coffeepot, and when he had the necessary money, he bought a ticket on the *Floreana*, not in the same class as the tourists, but rather in the class where the settlers traveled. When he entered the cabin that Iridia had long ago occupied, he felt a faint, familiar presence. The voyage was slow and sorrowful. For the tourists it was a tour; for the very few colonists that occupied the compartments close to the engines, it was a tedious, obligatory movement, the displacement of the meek in search of a bit of land where they could settle down and sink roots. The boat, well situated in the Humboldt Current, moved quickly for some. For others it seemed as if the sea had stretched as it stretched for Columbus, or perhaps it seemed that the islands had moved to another location.

Occupied with his own sorrows, Alirio was unaffected by scientific matters or by the transmutations he was going to see in the flora and fauna, nor was he interested in the historical suppositions discussed on deck as to whether so-and-so had wanted to buy the handful of islands in 1895 for four million pounds sterling for the benefit of England, or if Vacas Galindo proposed their alienation in 1905, or about whether in the construction of the Panama Canal, Alfaro had entertained the possibility of leasing them for ninety-nine years, in exchange for fifteen million dollars, or if General Villamil's cables had been broken by now by the biting sharks, sharks that Alirio looked at without seeing and without caring that in these latitudes they had even lost their bloodthirsty ugliness and instead appeared slender, elegant, elastic, as tame as the dolphins, far from the embodiment of evil and the curse of Moby Dick.

Alirio was at that time thirty-some years old. He had not seen the sea since he was a boy. He had always lived surrounded by mountains and dedicated to his poems. He had a confused notion of the ocean and a hazy vision of sharks with their two rows of sharp teeth, of the jellyfish that cause unbearable stinging, of the sunburns, of the gigantic waves that carry the unwary out to sea, of the crabs that bite one's big toe, of Venus emerging from a shell as in Botticelli's painting, of the legendary sirens trying to deceive Ulysses, of the blue, deeper than the blue of the sky... so that when Alirio drew close to the real sea of the islands, his astonishment rose in a crescendo and he once again felt the spiritual shaking that came of sensing material things, that feeling of being somehow transported to the stratosphere, that ability to capture the entire universe. The sea was simply imponderable, the sea was big... big... big... and it seemed impossible, but he could think of no other adjective, still less an incipient metaphor, never mind a logical association of ideas. Desperate, he opened his eyes wide, he beat his head with his hands, he pinched himself all over. He felt a million strange sensations, as if there were a wasps' nest inside him, but he could not explain, or express, or translate the sensations. He was at the apex of aphasia and the vertex of agraphia.

The infinite immensity in motion, the contact of the breeze with his skin, the sight of the clear waters where it was possible to read any given chapter of ichthyology, the sun changing the color and tone of every possible shade of blue and green, silenced him still more completely. He thought that the contact of his hand with the pencil might overcome this painful constipation, this inactivity of the lyrical pancreas, might perhaps hurry along the process of uterine contractions so as to produce the birth, serving almost as forceps. He needed that stimulus to crack the shell of the egg and hatch the chick. He wanted to displace the anguish of his frustrated vocation and forget the inexpressible pain of knowing himself suddenly relegated from the easy chair of the privileged to the vulgar and anonymous bench of the shapeless masses. With an effort, he uncrumpled a sheet of yellowed waiting and after chewing on the ends of his ever-present pen, he wrote with trembling, rapid letters, with the tachycardiac's tachygraphy:

> *¡Oh sea,*
> *how pacific are your waters!*

And he couldn't go on. He was on foot when others went by car. He remained standing when everyone else sat down. Bewildered, without knowing what was happening. Dry, like the straw of the high grasslands. Blank, like a sheet of unlined paper. Then a great humiliation came upon him from afar, as if his critics and admirers—who numbered in the thousands—filled the decks from port to starboard, sat upon the ocean waters and even hung from the mainmast, mockingly witnessing his failure. A tremendous humiliation wrapped him from head to foot, like a foul stench, when he realized that the two minimal lines he had just written on the wrinkled paper, trembling with lyrical frenzy, where not the product of his own mind, but the hackneyed phrase that Vasco Núñez de Balboa supposedly uttered when he first glimpsed the peaceful Southern Sea. And as a further taunt, he saw the words printed in bold in the standard fourth grade history text he used in school. Furious, desperate, on the verge of tears and of insanity, he wrote a third line, in thick, rebellious letters:

Down with Balboa, damn it!

From force of habit, he put the paper away in his pocket, among the manuscripts that remained unfinished, among the half-dressed verses and those awaiting the definitive word, among those that were standing in line for their chance to enter the printer's shop.

After that, he refused to hear about anything more. The islands were heaps of volcanic soil emerging from the sea, the cliff rocks with their fanciful shapes were black, irregular stones; the majestic iguanas were wall lizards in a larger size, the albatross and the seagulls were just birds. Darwin was a jerk, the solitude of the ancient and esoteric world left him silenced forever. His muse had not only abandoned him, he was the definitive widower. He had made a long voyage in vain. His muse wasn't in the islands or anywhere else, she had left planet earth on the fastest rocket and now he wandered through the stratosphere as if he were a zombie. He wouldn't eat a bite, he walked dragging his feet under the huge weight of his despondency, defeated and lost, defenseless, stroking the skull, the clavicles, and the worn ilium of death, lying down with her and breathing her malodorous, maggoty breath.

Years later, when his posthumous works were published—because the fact that he suddenly fell silent did not diminish the importance of his work—his astonished readers and critics read without understanding the epilogue to his voluminous work:

> *Oh, sea,*
> *how pacific are your waters!*
> *Down with Balboa, damn it!*

And they concluded, the most perceptive of them, that perhaps Alirio was entering the terrain of protest poetry, and perhaps he was taking a political stand when he went crazy in the savage solitude of the islands.

In reality, Alirio went crazy from sorrow and impotence. He cried because his muse had abandoned him forever. The idea—brutal, but possible—that she might have gone off with another only aggravated his suffering.

Jealousy penetrated his soul as if it were made of pumice and his body could go no further with that poor worm-eaten soul. He was an animal trapped in the most ignominious of cages, he was a degraded wreck who loved and hated at the same time and with the same vehemence. He was entirely destroyed, and now without his papers on his person, his true feebleness was evident, with his ribs exposed and his vertebrae like suspension points along his dirty shirt, barely supporting the lowercase *o* of his empty, tormented head.

His life had neither reason nor purpose. Lacking determination, he killed himself by slow, uncomfortable degrees, drinking day and night in the Three Chinamen tavern. He was often overtaken by genuine fits of rage that ended in sobs. It was heartbreaking to see him crying over the absence of the ingrate. He wasted away minute by minute, without remedy or recourse, and he lost himself in the dark labyrinths of alcohol and drugs, unable to come up with even the most basic of comparisons, unable to say: as white as snow, as blue as the sky, as green as grass or as spinach.

One day he glimpsed a woman walking quickly who had the hair and the black eyes of his muse—his muse, whom he had never seen! It was Iridia who passed him, balancing on her head a bundle of freshly laundered clothes. She maintained the balance of the bundle with the swaying of her hips and the rhythm of her feet that seemed not to touch the ground. For Alirio, the alcohol instantaneously evaporated and his brain shook itself with a spasm of neurons, throwing aside his intellectual drowsiness. He recognized his muse in her, because as soon as he saw her he felt moisture in the midst of his drought, he was awake and alert. He looked for the paper that he didn't have and so as not to let the inspiration that came to him from he didn't know where get away, he threw himself down on the burning sand and wrote with a fingernail:

> *Woman, for you the fountain resumed its flow*
> *crucible where sex...*
> *philosopher's stone of my...*
> *found, encountered, pursued...*

These were the first words, the first impressions that had occurred to him in over six months. Staggering and trembling in the middle of the street, right there, in front of everyone, on the sand that held the sun's severity, he caught her by the skirt and said, out of his mind and nearly breathless, because after writing what he wrote, he had to run to catch her: "For the love of God, woman, marry me!"

Iridia looked at him the way one looks at a little worm. With a rolling twist of her body she tried to get away from the pleading hand, saying without anger or disdain, "You don't even know who I am or what my name is."

"I don't care about your name. Your name is Poetry."

"Poetry! Ha! My name is Iridia."

And she went away laughing softly like the whisper of the sea breeze or the crackle of the waves on the beach. Alirio went back to what he had written in the sand, and there, kneeling, he remained for the rest of the day. He was enraptured, he had finally found her. He would once again write immortal verses. His overcast sky opened up and a ray of hope halted his flirtations with the bony one who felt in the full length of her bones the uneasiness of the most humiliating brush-off.

The next day, Alirio was a new man. He put aside the drink that had swamped the archive of his dull ideas. He shaved the sparse, pointed beard that made him look like an upside-down ear of corn. He took a dip in the sea, while the frightened fish moved to one side. He changed his clothes. He shook off his humiliating stagnation. He passed a rag over his dusty thoughts and, whistling the old tango, *Adiós muchachos, compañeros del olvido*, went out in pursuit of rehabilitation.

He began at the beginning, looking for work, accepting with bowed head the divine curse of eating bread by the sweat of his brow. Some time earlier, San Pío Pascual, moved to pity by his sadness and his prestige, which had followed him to the islands like a sorry dog, had proposed him as the announcer for a newly inaugurated radio station. Santa Livina had hit the roof, saying he was a miserable, sinning drunkard, but Brigita had interceded, saying that work cures the ills of both body and soul, and that if he wanted to she could give him a treatment with the miraculous infusion of the seven spirits, and Miss Estenia, teacher at the Genoveva de Brabante School, had said that everyone bore the moral obligation to help him to reform himself because—on top of everything else—they were talking about an intellectual who had published many books and could be a good teacher at the school.

So when Alirio showed up with a new sparkle in his eye, he started to work that very day, and his voice went out on the airwaves of all the islands, combining in a well-modulated and convincing tone the pyramids of Egypt with the Republic of Mauritania; the Grito de Dolores with the Sargasso Sea; the astronauts' trip to the moon with Berenguela, daughter of the king of Castile; the life of the marine and the land iguanas with Plato and dialectics; the Humboldt Current with the invention of the daguerreotype; the Platt Amendment with the men of the Renaissance. The musical background of his preposterous disquisitions and announcements followed a different path. It had nothing to do with what he said but rather with his state of mind; he could not put aside his sadness because Iridia had not even noticed his existence. The background music was tirelessly the same and was repeated over and over like an echo of the loneliness in which he was wasting away.

At first, the islanders, frozen between novelty and amazement, froze their radio dials as well, but little by little they tired of being unable to understand a word of what he was saying. They grew bored with the same scratched and tearful *pasillo* that hurried the tourists to their yachts.

Once again salsa and *guarachas* could be heard from the jukeboxes, playing more vigorously than ever, and so as not to have their spirits saddened further, one night they made a bomb and placed it right on the radio transmitter. Then Alirio was left without listeners, without a microphone and without work. Santa Livina rubbed her hands contentedly and San Pío Pascual rolled his eyes back until they looked like two big consecrated hosts, all the time nodding his head and repeating his refrain: "*O tempora, o mores.*"

"They have ostracized me," Alirio admitted, listless and hurt. He continued to observe Iridia's comings and goings, seated at the bar in the Three Chinamen, in front of a glass of orangeade, which he substituted for alcohol once he learned that she detested drunkards. Absorbed hour after hour in the color of the juice, he kept turning over and over the metaphysical question of the crucible of sex and the philosopher's stone that was Iridia, without managing to complete or to fix even one more line, or poem, or metaphor. Iridia, full of other thoughts and other sorrows, remained indifferent to the drama.

One fine day, Alirio woke up with a kind of tickle of inspiration. He hurriedly looked for his sheets of paper, he sharpened a pencil and went to sit down at a rustic table beside the sea. He filled his lungs with the saltiness and when he was about to begin writing, his mind once again went blank. Embittered, he began to write—as if he were performing exercises in calligraphy with his small, slanted handwriting—the word *love* and other signs, like *Iridia, water, sea, sand,* that seemed to represent nothing yet had a kabalistic significance. He kept writing them, hundreds of times, until he had filled all of the sheets of paper he had left. He filled them front and back, decorating them with drawings and strange symbols.

Alirio wrote as if in fact his inspiration were dictating at a hundred eighty per minute, and when his hand became stiff and sore with what seemed a useless pastime, he crumpled the sheets of paper into little round balls that the wind carried away one after the other, without interruption, like a long line of white pigeons, like the basting of a mysterious needle, making its way between the thorny bushes and the thickets of palo santo, uphill, toward the interior of the island, up to Brigita's land that bordered that of San Pío Pascual and Santa Livina, and which had no fence because until then it had not been necessary, because the evil passions that were buried had not yet come to light. When the balls of paper reached the spot they were supposed to reach, they settled themselves among the rocks, making themselves comfortable on the burning red ground as if they were settling into a nest, and they began to grow damp and to change into water.

Neither Alirio nor anyone else in the world could have known that if those words were written five hundred seventy-two times, along with the drawings Alirio had added, under certain circumstances—which were the circumstances Alirio was experiencing—they acted like a kabalistic sign so that any desert, living rock or arid ground should be transformed into an oasis, in the same fashion as when the people of Prague wrote on a parchment the kabalistic name of God and put it into the mouth of the Golem—who was a gigantic man of mud made by the Jew Judah Low—and the Golem was transformed into a living man.

While the water oozed, gradually becoming an irregular flow, Alirio, with his head in his hands, cried his eyes out, consumed by grief before the failure of his inexplicably vanished vocation. Then the Parca showed up looking for company and she touched him with a finger. Alirio was wasted away to the point that his body began to diminish. Suddenly, he no longer looked at the line of the horizon but at most at the nearby beach with its lace of foam. He no longer had his elbows on the table, now it was his jaw that rested there. The pale one smiled, holding up her lower maxillar with her phalanges. Alirio looked like a three-year-old child. He no longer looked at the beach with its border of foam but rather only at the wood of the table, which had been warped by the force of the sun and the drizzle. His buttocks were no longer on the chair because he couldn't reach the table, so instead his shoes rested on the chair. And he was no longer a three-year-old child looking at the wood of the table, but instead a one-year-old boy who tried to reach the pencil so as to scratch the table, while the osseous one, flexing her pubis and her femurs, sat down a little closer. And now he was no longer a one year old, but instead an infant, and the chair and the suction of his fingers in his mouth made up his entire surroundings. He fell off the chair trying to find his balance while the skinny one, flexing her kneecaps, squatted down in the sand. And he was no longer a little baby of a few days old because he was diminishing unavoidably until he became a fetus unable to look because he had entered the fish stage. He began to gasp because the air suffocated him and he needed his liquid environment. And then he was no longer a fetus, but only an embryo, on which the eyes, the arms and legs, were barely sketched, and then the heart stopped beating, while the inevitable one, on hands and knees, stuck her nasal bone into the sand.

And he kept inescapably shrinking until he disappeared from the view of the people and of she who cannot be bribed, lost among the tiny bits of shell, under a disordered pile of papers, and under the papers there remained a viscous dampness, like semen, that shone for a few moments in the sun of that extraordinary afternoon, and then it disappeared totally and definitively just as Morgan and his terror of death had disappeared.

Alirio had exchanged his life for a spring, perhaps because he understood, at the last moment, that people were losing the need to slake the thirst that only poems can satisfy, because he understood that to write was the most solitary and selfish act, and he wrote to satisfy a sad necessity because he knew for a certainty that he would never be able to say anything new to anyone, but could at best reflect his own anguish and the anguish that others have sometimes felt.

Iridia

I ridia walked along the beach, watching the horizon as always and leaving footprints on the sand for the sea to erase, and every day her steps left their traces in the life of every man who crossed her path and whom time would take care of plunging into nothingness, but at least she lived after her own fashion. One day she saw a pile of papers being tossed on the breeze. She gathered them up and she realized that they were the poems Alirio had written before he arrived in the islands; she read them absentmindedly and liked them. She looked for the poet so as to give them back, but could not find him anywhere. And from then on, every evening when the calm arrived, she sat down beside the sea to read the poems, and she kept reading until she almost knew them from memory. Alirio's poems had a shocking solitude like her own solitude before she arrived in the islands, and a terrifying solitude like her solitude after Morgan's departure. They spoke of the search for love as if it were a fact more vital than its possession, and of the certainty that death was lying in wait on every corner. She slowly relinquished her sorrow, like one changing her skin and ceasing to be herself so as to be the complement of other people. Sometimes, she felt herself dying of tenderness when she saw a man approaching her, head bowed, and she would take his hand so as to hold it for a long time between her own. Iridia stroked his cheeks, kissed his eyelids, touched his body and trembled all over just imagining herself taking refuge in Morgan's arms, and she felt the heat of the flesh grazing her trembling skin and pouring the man's anguish into her ears. She would have liked to roll up her self so as to unroll it like a carpet and place it at Morgan's feet. But it was no use, no man resembled him and she had to wait for all of the men of the islands so as to, with all of them together, barely make do with a faint shadow of Morgan.

When mating season arrived, the air become more delicate and the breeze more playful, and the white gulls began the task of building their nests. They fluttered above the cliffs, carrying in their beaks bits of white coral with which to construct their nests. Patiently, lovingly, they placed them on the inaccessible rocks so that the single egg they managed to lay would keep its balance and not roll into the abyss. When the gulls finished their task, the coral nest shone in the sun, it refreshed the atmosphere and the sea slept so as to hear the gulls that sat down to brood with a coo that pierced the air and tickled the soul. Nothing in the world was as moving as that call, nothing so sad, nothing so desolate, so much the sob of the ocarina, so much the mother's lullaby, so much the old cradlesong, *mmm, mmm, mmm,* as tenderly sad as a chapter of *My Sweet-Orange Tree* that a tourist had let fall amidst the lava, and that Iridia found and read at one sitting crying over every page and feeling herself pushed, defenseless, into the far corner of tenderness.

Bruising the palms of her hands and skinning her knees on the rocks, Iridia climbed up to the heights to better hear the song of the gulls that was scored in the same scale and with the same notes as her sorrow. Listening to the gulls was the same as reading Alirio's intimate poems. Devotedly, she kissed the tiny bit of dust that remained of what once had been Morgan with his horror of death, which she carried with her always, hung around her neck in a tiny little box of Chinese menthol that took the place of a funerary urn.

There, alone on the cliff, her tears streaming, she called him at the top of her lungs, just as the gulls called their chicks, until his hand rested on her shoulder. It was what she would have wanted from other men but how, how to find company without sex, how to make them give her their tenderness if everything in life was no more than a surreptitious, silent, and organized struggle against masculine tenderness? Men who were not like Morgan had been educated with a genuine horror of showing their gentle side, because affection was a symbol of weakness and they still needed to live more before tenderness could be identified not only with women and children, so that it might be natural to see a man walking down the street, caressing a flower.

When her sorrow eased and she had emptied her load of pain, she went down to the town, downcast and transformed, to continue the rites of her self-imposed holocaust. She took off her clothes soaked with salt and offered herself to the men who lined up at her door. Buñuel's Viridiana was reborn in the islands and the men did not commit abuses but rather waited for her with the same composure and seriousness with which they had lined up, years before, in front of the posts of the church that was not yet built, on the eve of Maundy Thursday, to wash themselves of sin and attend the miracle of the Last Supper. But ever since San Pío Pascual and Santa Livina had arrived in the islands, men and women had lost that custom because with those two came the evil and malice of the mainland. Among the men who waited at Iridia's door there were none of the lubricious looks of desire, nor did one hear the words expected in houses of prostitution. It seemed they, too, observed the rite of the sublimation of sex, and in fact all of them were madly in love with Iridia. Without arriving at any kind of verbal agreement, she had communicated to them her mysticism: just as she gave herself to all, no one could claim her as his own; she was the common good of the islands, like the sea with its abundance of fish, like the fertile soil of the hills, and like Brigita's spring.

Iridia longed for a child to complete her life cycle on earth. She dreamt of the child that should have Morgan's green and enigmatic eyes, his robust constitution, his longevity, the gestures and the tastes of that most beloved man, but the child did not arrive and Iridia suspected that her sterility had to do with the installation of the Hot Cakes Bakery. She didn't know exactly how, she only suspected, traveling in pursuit of obscure speculations; she stopped eating the bread and she watched the movements of the flour from a distance, hating the presence of Richardson, the owner of the bakery. She had decided that she would live her life in the islands in her own way or she would burst like a poor little bubble, but she would not go on being what she was before she met Morgan and carried him around her neck.

When Iridia lived on the mainland, in the slum of the port where she met Morgan one night, she read a leaflet about a woman who was venerated by everyone. People held her as a saint. The two of them were even physically similar: they both had the pallor of sadness, the long hair and black eyes of Alirio's muse. So each of them performed miracles after her own fashion: because Iridia was a woman and the other was a saint. They said that the latter tore her flesh with hair shirts, flogged herself with thorny branches, sweated blood, she went crazy with love-pain and slept on the sharp ridges of the stones. Dead, with that transition that Morgan would not have known and that Alirio had not expected, she granted the impossibilities that the desperate asked of her, so that a child might be cured without doctors or medicines, or an absent one might return to occupy the space he had left vacant; that some stolen money might appear, satiating the thief's hunger, or that a canary might rise from the dead and intone its yellow trills; that a blind man might have a photographic camera placed in his dead retina... Iridia admired her and wanted to imitate her in her goodness and her simpleness, although she thought that God must be horrified by the spectacle of a creature covered in blood, overwhelmed with love, and in pain. God, all-powerful in his glory, should have the elegance of a great lord and the tastes of men of refinement.

Iridia wanted to go beyond what she was offered by way of a model. She felt sorry for the men distanced from their wives. Many of them had been sent to the islands to serve out a sentence, although the penal colony fell apart because the authorities realized that the place was better for tourism than for punishment. A few of the convicts escaped and hid in the highlands, determined to remain in that paradise, because once outside the environment that had pushed them toward crime, they had reformed; they

loved freedom, valued the price they had paid for that
freedom, and were able to appreciate the beauty of the
wide sea. In the islands they had found themselves, they
had been purified of the vices of civilization, and although
they were consumed by idleness and tedium under the
blazing sun, they passed the time sitting on the rocks of
the cliffs, watching the horizon, waiting for some ship that
might bring them a letter or an outdated newspaper so as to
see the world, from a distance, affirming themselves more
all the time in their world of sand. The hundreds of tourists
who came and went every day mattered little to them. The
native men were few, but they had a definite personality:
they had learned to enjoy the pleasure of looking, unhurried,
at the souls of things. They had discovered the secret that
things had souls and that to discover that soul might take
years. They didn't know how to write like Alirio, but had
they known, they would have described new worlds.

Iridia lived in sadness because she could not find those
worlds. She could not find a sedative for her sorrow, she
ran away from herself bit by bit. She tried to save herself,
taking up the thread of tenderness. She wanted the men to
feel as she did, she wanted to give them another dimension
of the flesh. Perhaps she alone, defenseless and tiny, could
combat the heroes of film and television and above all those
absurdly masculine comic book heroes. She had never met a
man who hadn't wished, from the time he was a child, to be
Superman, so incapable of a caress; who had not dreamed
of being Batman, so incapable of loving deeply; who had

not identified with Dick Tracy, so incapable of kissing with
that hard, hard wooden mouth; who had not dreamed of
changing into Spiderman, Captain Lightning, the Comet,
the Lone Ranger and so many others, so unable to succumb
to love, to romance, to the tender tear. And now, no longer
boys but men, they identified still more with the heroes
who would cease to be heroic if they showed themselves to
be sweet or sensitive, and they hid their softness in public
life because it was a stain on their role as leaders. Who
ever saw Fidel Castro in love? Public men displayed their
conquests, not their fidelity, and when one appeared who
didn't mind being photographed holding hands with his
girlfriend, at best he was low-balled as a good man, which
was all but equivalent to weak man. Because of this, Iridia
came up with the crazy idea of staying in the islands, trying
to awaken masculine tenderness from its slumber.

The tourists said that the islands were inhabited by lazy
people who didn't want to build adequate hotels for their
needs, but the men of the islands were neither laborers
nor masons, they were born philosophers with their own
scale of values, the opposite of that established by those
who lived subject to civilization and were less happy. The
people of the islands looked at the tourists as if they were
watching a parade of ants dressed in motley, and although
they left some of their cursed money in the islands, they
were only ghosts who could not be taken into account. It
was said that the settlers neither sowed nor reaped, but
the truth was that they were very busy ordering things

according to the color and size of their souls, souls that only they could see and classify, so they were happier than city folk because they lived apart from cars and noise, apart from pseudo-liberated, stylish women, apart from conventionality and prejudice, from mass standardization and a life of absurdity.

Iridia would have liked to be like the Samaritan woman, but the men did not ask her for water. They asked water of Brigita; of Iridia, they asked only her body. But when she gave herself to them, she gave only the smallest part of her being. She could not give herself entirely, because to do so would have destroyed them, and because she had given herself entirely to Morgan's memory. She gave herself to the men with boundless compassion. She was the prostitute who gave and did not take. She showed herself just as she was—just the opposite of women who hid behind masks of hypocrisy, who joined their hands in an attitude of prayer, like a praying mantis, that hid the powerful pincers with which they caught the male so as to swallow him. She was not one of those who took shelter under male prestige so as to be other than they were. She was not one of the sluts who seized a position by inventing a baby as bait, or those who gave themselves for sport with no ethical solidarity toward their own sex, or who gave their flesh without love and without being spurred on by poverty. Iridia was beyond the common woman.

The men of the islands loved and also respected her. Each encounter was something more than the union of microgametes and macrogametes. Iridia awaited the child that was taking its time in coming and that would be hers alone. Each body was the body of Morgan, who would be the father of her child. She dreamt of him and mourned because she knew that, weighed down by the secret of the treasure that would remain forever buried, he did not rest in peace. Iridia read Alirio's poems avidly and looked for peace at the remotest horizons and in the irreconcilable extremes of purity and sex, of solitude and company, of the living and the dead, of men and the native creatures, of light and shadow. She shared her life out between suffering and work, and while her work was repudiated over where Santa Livina lived and on the mainland, those men who approached her for the first time, oozing with lust, when they touched her, they stopped in confusion, remembering immediately a girlfriend or an absent wife, and often they left with their desire lax and frozen and, without saying a word, they went to sit down at the edge of the sea, filled with an unfamiliar dignity. They remained unmoving for hours, and their heads had the majestic grandeur of the stones of Easter Island, looking at what only they could see and thinking about the privilege it was to live in the islands, because only there could these never before experienced situations occur. It seemed as if the people had washed and purified themselves and were better because they had banished from their lives all remnants of selfishness; they lived in a state of goodness, free of the vices of the mainland. They did not want to have anything more, they were themselves and they did not run anywhere; and without anyone offering them any sort of explanation, they knew that they were in possession of the truth because they enjoyed glimpsing the souls of things and they were in the ranks of the blessed, pure of heart.

Iridia did not live in the islands but rather in heaven, and she was seated at the right hand of God the Father, All-Powerful. When she came down to earth to give herself to men, she came with sanctifying grace and with the power of all charismata. She perceived from a distance the nature of the men with whom she was going to have contact. They had to be clean as she was, with a purity of spirit similar to that of the sea lions who mated to the rocking of the waves, under a sky purified by light. They must be similar to the tortoises hatching their eggs, slowly and conscientiously. They must be like the white gulls and have the sweetness of their song that brought tears to the eyes.

Iridia worked her tenderness, knowing that she had to protect and teach it like a young animal, like the plants that she watered, picking off the dry leaves because later, her solitude would enclose her in its iron circle; when human beings began to fail her, she would have to cling to things and when people failed her completely, she would begin to talk to other beings. The cacti, the *orchillas* and even the mantas would know her dreams and her longings and would grow taller than ever, but before going on in that way, with that emotional relationship from the human to the vegetal, she would die, for death with its teeth would cut the cord on the weaker side.

The men of the islands who went to Iridia might resemble any animal, save the cormorants with their reddish black color, heavy and indolent birds who had forgotten how to fly. One day, with so much fish in their claws, they stopped taking flight and remained stuck to the earth. They lost their wings and sprouted ridiculous little flippers, poorly covered with hairy feathers. Thus, when a man unworthy to touch her arrived at her home, Iridia guessed that he was a cormorant and without saying a word, she closed her eyes, contracted her body, and concentrated her mind. Her muscles grew as tense as the carob trees on her patio. They acted like a huge catapult and expelled the unworthy, throwing him into bottomless space through her window.

Often, the good people of the town would see the drunken sailors, the thieving merchants, the adulterous males, and the officers of the military base where the bony one was lodged go flying through the air. Iridia felt so sorry for the conscripts, young things immodestly shorn and with an absent gaze who were hired out to unload boats full of merchandise, to build mansions, and to cut roads, marring the face of the islands. Iridia hated the military commanders who trafficked in the muscles and sweat of those who had been tricked, who still believed in the fatherland and were being used. The stultifying, endless daily routine to which they were subjected pained her. Each dawn she awoke, startled, and she was unable to get back to sleep from the moment they passed by her house shouting deafeningly thousands upon thousands of times, up to infinity:

> *one, two, find your shoe, three, four, out the door,*
> *one, two, find your shoe, three, four, out the door...*

Iridia was upright and authentic. Her window had no glass, only a printed cloth curtain that moved with the unceasing gusts of the sea breeze as if it were life's standard. She knew that the islands were an expression of freedom and cleanliness. She had everything there, although she had nothing. They were the opposite face to the environment where she was born and grew up surrounded by neglect and poverty, the poverty that appears alongside the scraps left by opulence. She would never be able to erase from her memory the stifling winters when the heat grew in sudden blazes and it stopped raining water to rain crickets instead—the fat crickets that slammed into the floor and the walls producing a muffled *plop, plop*. She would never be able to forget how one night, when she lay down on the poor bed she had on the mainland in which she used to cover herself up to her hair with the sheet so as to isolate herself from the shack, after taking the usual precautions, she began to stretch out and she stretched and stretched until her feet reached the shadow of terror and ran into something soft, nervous, and hot.

Terrified, she curled up on herself while her body's adrenaline secreted cold sweat from fear. An animal or a demon was lodged in her very own bed. Her hair stood on end as if terror itself were tugging it toward the darkness, and she remained paralyzed when the lump that her feet had touched emerged, dragging itself across her naked body, leaving her with the harsh contact of its feet, its claws, and its tail which seemed to have no end, and then it paused very close to her face in a confrontation of two opposing worlds. Malevolent little eyes fixed on her terrified eyes and they looked at each other for a fraction of the centuries in which the ancient terror of the mystery of evil, of the kabala of the dark, of depthless anguish was conceived, born, and matured; not fear of sin, which is the ruse of power, but rather of the subhuman depths of perversion, of the place frequented by the pale one who carried off little children and young mothers.

Then the genie of the darkness took a tremendous leap, which was almost a flight, and disappeared into the shadows of the night. Iridia learned nothing more, because ever since then, people and things had changed their natural way of being. She found that within everything that existed there was for her a hidden depth of wickedness, that evil seemed to exist in all things, crouching, ready to spring upon her.

That night, Iridia's mother and siblings were awakened, astonished, by the uncontainable laughter produced by Iridia's body, a body bathed in tears. The others started to laugh, too: laughter was so unheard of in the middle of the night or by light of day in that miserable house. But little by little, the others tired of laughing, and when her mother went to tell Iridia to be quiet so as to get back to sleep, she stopped cold. Her daughter was not laughing out of happiness, she was dying of laughter. The light of dawn caught her still laughing, while she tried to indicate a certain spot, and when they got up, they looked and found the reason for the tremulous laughter; they saw, crouched in a corner of the split bamboo walls, terror also escaping from its small fearful eyes, balancing on the edge of instinctive insanity and concentrating all the agility of a cornered animal for the acrobatic leap, the enormous black rat: rat of depthless evil, rat bristling with bubonic plague, rat of sewers and misery into which the bony one had entered so as to remind Iridia that she was hers.

In the midst of the shouting, the neighbors trapped the rat. They killed it with sticks, beat the stuffing out of it without compassion, and threw it into the estuary. But Iridia kept laughing and she kept on that way for three days until the slum's local healer searched determinedly for a broody hen from which she took an egg, and with it she rubbed Iridia's whole body, praying—professionally—a credo. The *espanto*, the spirit of fright, finally left her convulsing body and settled in the center of the yolk. The old woman's gnarled hands picked up the egg carefully, she blew on the shell a few times and she put it into a jar that held rocks. Staggering, she climbed into a canoe, rowed a zig-zag course out to sea, and threw the jar into the depths. She returned without looking back, dignified and plain, and only when she put her hand on Iridia's forehead did she declare the cure complete. But Iridia had already seen and felt the dark side, she had come face to face with death and seen the threat in her eyes.

When Iridia felt better and had recovered her strength, there was a new gleam in her eyes; the neighborhood kids called and she went out to play apathetically on the old, eaten-away boards that served as bridges across the stagnant waters. The children stopped playing when they saw a bird appear, fluttering over their heads. The evening shadows were falling and the bird, feeling itself pursued, took refuge in Iridia's house. No bird had ever been seen thereabouts. It flew between the extended arms and the trembling fingers that tried to capture it. Iridia stood on a chair and managed to catch it. Imprisoned in her fist, she felt the beat of a small heart, she was going to give it a kiss on the beak to calm it down and then return it to its nest, but when she looked at it, the bird had lost the beak it never had and in its place there was a long, drooling snout and a pair of little eyes similar to those of the rat that had crouched in her bed. Iridia felt herself the prey of death, she opened her hand and fell down in a faint. The bird continued its journey toward the darkness, while the well-meaning neighbor ladies tried to revive the inanimate body. It was no bird that had lost its nest, but instead a disgusting bat, with the same malignant, triangular face and the very same cruel little eyes. Years later, when Iridia arrived in the islands and ran into Santa Livina, she realized that the rat, the bird, and Santa Livina were too much alike, the three had the same searching gaze, eager to penetrate the forbidden territory of conscience, to cut off lives and happiness. Santa Livina, with her thin and hoity-toity figure, contrasted with the trembling, sybaritic flesh of her nephew. With her claw-like index finger, with her severe austerity that colored everything she touched black, with her hatred of sex that never for an instant left her dirty mind, she infused the air of the islands with sin. Iridia knew then that the black rat returning from the darkness had been reincarnated in the bat, sent by death to remind her that she had a date. There was a reason people insisted that old, decrepit rats sprouted wings and that flies turned into spiders and that those who had seen death up close would never be happy again.

The bony one was stalking Iridia, she needed to travel far away and save herself. It was then that Morgan appeared in her life and for him she left the mainland. In the islands a breastplate of light protected her. Life and death waged bitter battles over her head. She didn't know that. She believed herself free because she was far from the miserable, sordid environment of the slum with its rotten miasmas that thickened the air; far from the harsh, bitter cries of the neighborhood women who had to unburden themselves to the wind; far from the raids that the brutal, all-encompassing police organized, hunting the street-walking mothers who sought shelter in vain at the entrance to the temples, and who should have left the profession to the real prostitutes—women who didn't need to sell their bodies, because they did it for free, coldly and professionally, calculating every step, every peso, every kiss and who schemed a child in their insides so as to forge new alliances and destroy others. With a misunderstood women's liberation, the times in which it was Iridia's lot to live had changed: they were no longer the times when the brutal macho got the poor woman pregnant; instead they were times in which the female, reincarnated as a praying mantis, got children off of the poor man.

In the islands, the finches landed in flocks for the midday meal and they stood on the edge of Iridia's plate, pecking at the same rice that she ate, and they told her about their flights through the air, about the growth of their chicks, and about everything that could be seen from the heights. Iridia felt herself in glory when she exchanged the sordid misery of the slum for the mild poverty of her house shaken by waves and by wind, and she had to somehow pay her debt to life. She didn't need the treasure that Morgan had wanted to bequeath her, she only needed his presence, because their love, painfully unrealized, was a torment.

One day she felt an overriding, vehement urge to go to the place where Morgan had disappeared. No sooner had she arrived than she saw, to her surprise, that a ray of sunlight had driven itself into the ground at the same spot where her lover's body had disintegrated. It seemed like an arrow that proclaimed possession of a territory. She touched the ray of sunlight and found it solid as transparent iron; it was solid as a golden reed, strong as a celestial rail, clear as a blade of glass. It was tempting to stand and then walk on it because it sloped like an ascending ramp, and when Iridia did so she saw the inevitable skinny one come running, out of breath, hopping between the rocks and leaving shreds of her black rags among the *orchillas* and the spines of the cactus, and she moved up their date. Iridia began to ascend the celestial ramp. The one who blinds managed to touch her foot. Iridia might have lost her balance, but a supernatural force was carrying her obliquely upwards towards the center of the sun, with the mechanism of an automatic staircase. Iridia was light and she kept walking; she was slowly gaining altitude like a weightless figure from the brush of Marc Chagall. From time to time she paused to breathe and reestablish her balance, although she knew that her shoes had sprouted soft suction pads that stuck to the ray, which was the same one that trapped the white butterfly that emerged from Morgan's foot and that illuminated the viscous dampness, like semen, that had been Alirio.

Iridia climbed contentedly, saying goodbye to the inhabitants of the islands, to the white gulls that made her cry, to the finches who told her about their lives, to the albatross and the mockingbirds, to the centipedes and the dolphins, to the spiders and the sea lions, and while she climbed, she began at last to see the true soul of things along with the desperation of the bony one who never took into account the possibility that she might find this path.

In all the islands, only three people saw her. Brigita,

who crossed herself with one hand while she waved her handkerchief with the other, saying goodbye and advising her to watch her step, that she mustn't fall, and to remember her. Miss Estenia, who went to look for the school's telescope to see if it pierced the bulk of the clouds so as to be able to tell the children the story. And San Pío Pascual, who was left breathless and had to lie down on his back until she was lost to sight, and when Santa Livina wanted to see what he was looking at, she could only make out a moving dot. She grimaced in disgust and her sole comment was, "The sky is growing cobwebs."

San Pío Pascual didn't dare tell her that it was Iridia walking in the sky, afraid that she would tell him he was crazy, that he was senile and that he was being contaminated with the animal sensuality that Iridia awakened in the men who came near her. But she ordered him to get up, because that was no way for a priest to watch the spiders that were up in the clouds.

Fritz

He didn't eat, he didn't drink, he didn't sleep; he wasn't consumed by the vulgar love of common mortals, but by the sacred fire of science. Sometimes, when he woke up in a sensitive mood, he realized that the master classes he taught at the university, classes into which he poured all a lover's passion, were deathly boring for his students, who had other interests and other loves. It was as if he were talking to a cement wall, but that mattered little: he enjoyed talking to himself, hearing with delight the scientific terms that only he understood, asking himself difficult questions and answering with irrefutable arguments. He perceived, without it bothering him one little bit, the way his students used the back rows to escape. Relentlessly, and with no attempt at disguise, the classroom gradually emptied. The echo assured him that he cast his pearls before swine, confirming his view of himself as a sage.

When he was at home, his wife, tired of dressing as if she had nothing on—because all of her clothes fit tight as a glove—and tired of undressing at night as if she were performing the dance of the seven veils for an audience of experts, fed up with exciting him as if she were a Nabokovian Lolita, up to here with trying to seduce him as if she were the most professional of whores and tired of using her extremities and other parts of her body as a fishing line to catch him again, had relegated him at last— after years—to sleeping in the guestroom, where Fritz and the circles under his eyes wandered about from dusk until dawn, thinking about the *Opuntia echios*. Encapsulated within his own rapture as if he were inside a cyst, he was hopelessly in love with science.

Fritz was the greatest researcher of prickly pears in the world, and though he had written and published numerous reports that shook the restricted world of botany, he still needed to investigate a few more details in order to bring to a conclusion his great contribution to the plant world. He had spent many years of his youth in the islands, cutting sections and cross sections of the fleshy leaves, measuring the size of the spines and the distance between each one of them as well as each one's relation to the center of the leaf and to the petiole. He had weighed and analyzed the quantity of liquid each leaf contained, broken down the chemical nature of the stalks and the roots, counted how many spines there were on a leaf, how many on a plant, how many in a square meter of ground and how many in all of the islands.

At some point, he had married and had children, but as he knew neither how nor when, he had not the remotest notion of the process or of the metamorphosis of love into sex. He could almost have believed that babies came from Paris, but as the children existed, and had to be fed and educated, he gave himself over to the devil and to neuroses before the demands of economic necessity. Until at long last, at the end of a few years' span that to him seemed centuries, he was able to take a break from his pedagogical labors. He planned a trip to the dreamed-of islands that would last a glorious few months—which in other words meant he would be alone with his beloved beside the sea.

This time, he would make the crossing by plane so as to save time and not by ship as on previous trips, when he had been interested in studying the influence of ocean currents on the *Opuntia echios*. He felt happy and euphoric, like a man going to love's first tryst. He felt twenty years younger. He hummed in the shower, he smoothed his bristling moustache in front of the mirror, he combed his gray hair, while his scorned wife burned with envy and indignation knowing that she couldn't even confront or fight her rival because at most she had seen her on the covers of his books and in a large painting that presided over his work table: she was white, fat, and Rubenesque, she was seated among and on top of books, dossiers, and scrolls, with a white Grecian tunic that scarcely contained the stampeding escape of two voluminous breasts. His wife didn't even know her whereabouts, she knew only that she was an exacting woman, as demanding and intractable as a luxury-model mistress.

No sooner had Fritz received the ticket sent to him by a foreign institution than he packed his bags with whatever he found to hand. But his notes and personal observations he stored orderly and methodically in various numbered folders, and with all of them under his arm and with his pack on his back, he set off for the airport without saying goodbye to anyone, not out of thoughtlessness but due to an involuntary forgetfulness, which shattered those feeble conjugal relations that should never have existed in the first place. He arrived as if floating on air, taking tiny steps as if he wanted to dance a minuet with that bare-breasted woman, but his wide smile shrank to a grimace of annoyance, puckered up like an anus, when he sensed that he was going to have problems. It was evident—even to his congenital absentmindedness—that the number of passengers going to the islands was greater than the number that would normally fit in the plane that was ready to take off.

Packed together boisterously in the waiting lounges

and the corridors, an enormous group of tourists from the four corners of the earth waited to board the plane that would carry them to the Enchanted Isles. The sounds of the Tower of Babel rose from the group in every variety and accent. Beside them, a group of five men remained absorbed in their reading, their plane tickets peeking out of their jacket pockets, while the usual women, habitually found in airports, buzzed and fluttered around them, attracted by the flash of the society page journalist who had shot them from several different angles without the men taking the least notice. The women smelled prestige; self-absorption, baldness, grayness didn't matter. It was perfectly evident that the five were not tourists. From time to time they would look at the plane that still hadn't warmed up its engines, and they impatiently consulted their watches before once again burying themselves in their reading.

When Fritz arrived, he panned across the heads, stopped to focus on the five men, and resolutely walked toward them. They looked at each other, sniffing one another affectionately; they exchanged names and shared a fraternal embrace, since one way or another, they had heard of each other due to the affinity of their work.

Their names coincided in the same scientific journals. Their circles of action overlapped, and although they were in love with the same woman, they were not rivals but colleagues. Professor Fritz brought to their attention what they would never have imagined for themselves, namely the quantity of people who were going to travel to the same place. The scientists, who came from far-off Denmark, understood nothing; patting the pockets where they kept their tickets, they seemed to say: this has nothing to do with us. Fritz, more familiar with the area, deflowered their respective understandings, explaining to them—breathless with indignation—what was evident, and he began to protest the inappropriate over-sale of tickets. The scientists, out of sentimental affinities and intellectual interests that were also evident, joined him in the protest, forming an invulnerable bloc of force and logic. They meticulously closed their folders, carefully folded and packed their ideas, stored their reading glasses in their cases, and stood up behind the professor.

Each of them surpassed in height and weight even the most well-built tourists. After a to and fro between the airline ticket counter and the immigration counter, and from the latter to the information desk, they realized that no one wanted to take responsibility for anything. Then, after a short whispered consultation in which the bald heads came together like a bunch of grapefruits, and without waiting for the agreed-upon signal from the loudspeakers: *Passengers with the destination Galápagos Islands, board at gate number...* Nothing more was heard, the Danes and Fritz with their folders of notes under their arms and their packs on their backs opened a path through the tumult, crossed the threshold of the exit door and, at a victor's pace, headed for the plane. The guards, naturally, tried to stop them, but they pushed aside guards and flight attendants with swift blows of their packs, swinging at point-blank range and shouting stentoriously as if they were going to war: *Make way for Science!* They climbed the stairs to the plane that shuddered above the asphalt as if the feet of the invaders produced an allergic reaction. They placed in the hand of the startled flight attendant their respective tickets. They settled themselves in the forward seats, behind the cockpit. They adjusted their respective seatbelts. They opened their thick files of notes, unfolded their ideas and smoothed them out, and they became absorbed in the facts that interested them, divinely indifferent to the tumult that they had left at their backs.

Given the enormous prestige that a bad example has always enjoyed among the masses, everywhere and all over, the rest of the impatient tourists, seeing with their own eyes what the decided group of scientists had done—led by Professor Fritz and his moustache, which trembled in time to his steps—tried to do the same, but the police quickly mobilized, believing that a hijacking was underway. The reflexes of all the guardians of order were synchronized; they closed the doors, they released the safeties on their rifles and fine-tuned their aim. The hundreds of passengers who remained inside, feeling themselves passed over and discriminated against, began to demand their rights.

The captain of the ship arrived, cap in hand, to see what was happening to his plane, and when they explained to him the treachery, he tried to calm their spirits. He said that another plane was ready and that, for the moment, only fifty passengers could board, but all of them displayed their tickets for the plane that supposedly should have been in the clouds at least an hour ago. The pilot nervously wrung his cap and upbraided the sales manager. The sales manager nervously reviewed the endless list of passengers and upbraided the reservations agency over the phone. The reservations agents, in their respective offices, upbraided their innocent secretaries. The innocent secretaries defended themselves telephonically, saying that the boss had told them that... The boss said it wasn't true, because he had ordered the assistant manager to... The assistant manager said that was on Monday, because the manager had said that... The manager said that he had spoken to the assistant manger on Tuesday and that he was a... The assistant manager said that on Wednesday, in the closed meeting, it had been agreed that... And the whole thing was a brazen and unprecedented passing of the hot potato across telephone lines that were on the verge of short circuiting, while the airport authorities tried to draw away a bull with a hundred thousand horns.

The pilot put on his cap, which had lost its usual shape, and when he put it on, it covered his ears. Almost without seeing where he was going, he headed for the plane, chewing on a litany of swearwords, and when he climbed in, he confronted the six men who were sprawled in their seats, peacefully reading. Without any sort of consideration, he called them everything from hijackers to undesirable foreigners, which was the strongest thing he could possibly say after having taken a course on promoting tourism. He spat categorically that he would not travel in their company, and the undesirable foreigners replied that they would not leave his little airplane because they were within their rights and that if they didn't take off immediately, they would sue the company for damages, because they didn't travel for pleasure, as the others did, they traveled sent by their respective research institutes to carry out serious and urgent studies and every minute that passed was inexcusable. Naturally, the one who spoke with such energy was Professor Fritz, who burned with desire to keep his date with the *Opuntia echios* that would be his pretext to sink into the arms of the bare-breasted woman. The others were somewhere between embarrassed and sorry to have seconded him.

The pilot observed Fritz's obstinacy, which would not be moved even with the help of the police. He left the aircraft and strode with long steps from the plane to the waiting lounge, from the waiting lounge to the airline counter, from the airline counter to the control tower—and from the control tower, which was unable to give the order to depart because all of the telephones suggested they try their call again later, he didn't know where else to go; all this without finding any kind of solution.

The North American tourists, furiously chewing their gum, complained to the guide who could not explain to them exactly what was happening and only assured them that up until seven a.m. on the dot everything was perfectly planned and organized. The English quietly discussed among themselves the topics of colonialism and the politics of Third World countries. The Germans blocked the exit doors and took turns one by one telephoning their embassy personnel, and a group of Latinos brazenly opened their wallets and offered bribes to everyone so as to secure seats on the second aircraft which was destined for a flight to somewhere else.

At last, the second plane, after a long period of uncertainty and allegations of every kind, carried off the most disgruntled of them, beginning a period of relative calm.

In the first aircraft, the scientists, absorbed in their reading, didn't even notice that the others had taken the lead. The pilot, tired of arguments and threats, and having refused to travel with those who had taken his plane nearly by force, took off all his clothing, apart from the cap, and went to sunbathe on the control tower terrace, lying naked on his back in the same way that he did after each flight on the solitary beaches of the islands to which he had traveled uninterruptedly and without mishap until the day Fritz crossed his path.

Close to midday, when the scientists were about to explode, the expert in the *Buteo Galapagoensis*, doing honor to the hawks in which he specialized, picked up a tray and set himself to serving an improvised lunch to his companions who languished in hunger and impatience. He

soothed them with Coca-Cola and ham sandwiches. The
nourishment calmed the spirits of the five; not so Fritz,
who now had more energy to continue the fight. They ate in
silence as befit empty stomachs and strong tensions. Their
tremendous arousal abated a degree and as they saw that,
installed up there in the belly of the plane that burned as if
it were at the peak of digestion, the hours passed and passed
and they had no one before whom to raise a complaint, nor
did they need to leave the plane, they wisely made their
work plans for the day and set themselves to await the next
in company with an attractive flight attendant who had
received the order not to abandon the hijacked plane and
who, in the midst of so much confusion, had been forgotten.

Night came with its bundle of shadows and its suitcase
of cold. The flight attendant closed the door, made peace
with the scientists, and served them coffee. Fritz had fallen
into the blackest despondency. They drank the coffee,
taking sips of cordiality, and told of their experiences
on other trips without noticing that the expert in the
Diomedea irrorata, from the moment he boarded the plane
and handed his ticket to the startled flight attendant, had
felt a strange sensation. He had noted that she walked in
a very singular manner and that her pronounced buttocks
formed an acute angle in a way uncommon among humans.
As soon as he saw her, she seemed to him an albatross in
uniform. He thought her delightful and he thought that the
only thing she needed was to have white feathers all over
her body and above all a few longer feathers in her tail in

order to be perfect, absolutely perfect, far beyond purely human perfection. Perhaps her mother, her grandmother, or some other forebear had done something similar to what happened in the myth of Leda when Zeus became a swan in order to seduce her. The flight attendant had closed the door to keep out the cold. She was the most admirable bird-woman symbiosis, much more complete than the pious conjunction *Ave Maria* might be to one of the faithful. Each time she went to the rear of the aircraft, he watched her every step. In the click of her heels he thought he heard the snapping of beaks at the beginning of the courtship ritual. He watched her so much that he finally caught the beat of her walk. He began to move his head rhythmically from side to side, following the swinging of her hips, and to say softly, *go go go go*. The two seemed then a pair of albatross in the midst of courtship. The only thing that was out of place was that they were inside an airplane and not on the warm sands of the islands.

And it happened that because of these deep biological affinities, inexplicable to the uninitiated, out of so much watching her on his part and so much being watched on hers, they instantly became friends and then ardent lovers. Given the circumstances, when silent and concealing night fell, after the door was closed and they'd had their coffee, the other scientists maintained an uncomfortable silence at the extreme front of the aircraft while the expert in the *Diomedea irrorata* experienced the best moments of his life—unshakably celibate until that point—imagining that the two were already in the islands and feeling that they made the most beautiful pair of albatross ever seen in books of zoology or on tourist postcards.

But Professor Fritz, who was the symbol of fidelity, if not to his wife, then to the bare-breasted woman, was uncomfortable and irritated with everything that was happening at the rear of the plane. He was no moralist, but this kind of betrayal of the abstract woman pained him. In other circumstances, the fact would have gone unnoticed, but in such close contact, Fritz could not get to sleep. The other Danes, knowing the passion their colleague felt for the *Diomedea irrorata*, found the precise explanation of the erotic event; it did not take them by surprise, they took it as the continuation of an investigative project and they fell asleep peacefully, because they, too, had noticed that the flight attendant, despite not having feathers, was almost an albatross. She walked exactly as those birds did, due to the shape of her pointed glutei, and they saw not betrayal but, on the contrary, a confirmation that the love of science could produce such situations and many others as well, and they fell asleep at once, tired out by the tensions accumulated during the day. But as Fritz knew nothing of these antecedents, night for him became interminable, and to calm his insomnia, which had reared up stubbornly, and to entertain his thoughts and not think about what he considered a tremendous lack of respect among scientists of their stature, he set himself to inspecting the plane from top to bottom, and he observed many more irregularities, not of a sexual but of an aeronautical nature, which he took the precaution of writing down in his notebook. He tried to doze for a few moments, but was unable to find a comfortable position or to reach the calm that had settled around the other men and beside the couple intentionally avoiding their company.

The next day, when the sleepers began to awake and loosen up their atrophied muscles, the pilot appeared, freshly shaved, with a new cap, and more determined to enter into negotiations with those whom he had previously called hijackers. But they were haggard and in a bad way from being up all night and they had a new dose of sly aggressiveness, which they nonetheless managed to calm by making a conciliatory preamble. It seemed that the desired solution would result, that they would arrive at the necessary understanding and that they would be able to take off in the first hours of the morning, until the moment when Professor Fritz took out his notebook and said, like a person throwing a jug of cold water, which now seemed more like gasoline, onto a fire: "Your aircraft is a piece of junk."

The Danes were dumbfounded. The pilot leapt into the flames. Reacting violently, he said the most sensible thing he could say at that moment in which hostilities were renewed: "My plane is for flying, not for living in, the way you people are doing without permission."

Professor Fritz planted himself firmly so as to give more weight to his words and replied with all the weight of his bad night on his back, "For flying, ha! Your little airplane doesn't even have lifejackets and we're going to cross the Pacific Ocean."

At one bound, the captain reached the compartment where the lifejackets were kept and confirmed that, indeed, there were only three. Some forty-seven, give or take, were missing. Furious, he asked the flight attendant (who had returned to her usual role after her metamorphosis into a female albatross) where the lifejackets were and she replied, a bit ill at ease, looking at her fingers as if the lifejackets were rings, that she had no idea, that she didn't know...

"What do you mean, you don't know? They're all missing!" thundered the furious captain. There was an awkward silence in which the witnesses were just in the way and during which Fritz's stature, as if spurred, swelled rapidly. Recalcitrant and buzzing like a wasp, he hopped up and down as if to say, "Didn't I tell you? Didn't I tell you your plane is a piece of junk?"

The situation broke down completely. It was impossible to reach any sort of understanding. This time the stubborn one was the pilot, who refused to take off without the immediate appearance of the corresponding lifejackets.

Meanwhile, the tourists of the night before filled up a third aircraft and the waiting areas once again filled to the brim, and upon seeing that the first aircraft wasn't departing at the promised hour either, the shouting and the complaints began with such intensity that one would have thought there was a single plane in the entire world about to fly into the stratosphere just before an atomic bomb exploded. The tourists' desperation and anxiety increased by the minute in the midst of the disorder and confusion. The lifejackets were nowhere to be found. The scientists were dying of hunger and fatigue, they regretted seconding Fritz, and they said they didn't care a bit about the lifejackets and they would fly without them as they must have done many times before. Their work plans used up, they could not allow themselves the luxury of sitting with their hands folded. Everything that was happening was unprecedented, this was no longer a protest against a lack of organization, they were simply stunned by such perfectly organized disorganization.

At least the expert in the *Diomedea irrorata* was in heaven. He blessed his good luck and he blessed the country that had given him the opportunity to find his mate, with whom he had reached such a level of understanding that he didn't feel the passage of time or any discomfort, or even realize what was really happening, because he was going through an ecstasy that he had never felt before. After thinking hard about his situation, calculating the pros and cons of the exceptional circumstances, figuring and refiguring sums that always came out in his favor, savoring the syrup of true love and the encounter with the incarnation of one who had until that day been his lady and mistress, although a cold and distant spouse, he wanted to take the decisive step. Thinking, not with his refrigerated scientist's brain but with the ardent heart of a lovesick adolescent, he timidly approached the pilot and asked to speak to him alone, in confidence. The pilot thought he was going to reveal where the lifejackets were and led him, companionably taking his arm, to the cockpit.

The scientist, fixing the pilot with eyes of a blue and transparent ingenuousness, asked point-blank if he could marry them. The flight attendant waited modestly at the back. He had to repeat the question several times: could the captain marry the two of them: he, of legal age, marital status single, Danish by birth; and she, flight attendant by profession, marital status single, and native of this country, in the same way that the captain of a ship was authorized to perform marriages on the high seas, because in view of the circumstances, the need to formalize their commitment was imperative. The pilot, without answering him at all, began to curse his profession, the day of his birth, and the existence of the islands on the other side of the ocean.

Meanwhile, the rest of the tourists, tired of waiting in vain, planned to take by assault any other plane that might appear. The loudspeakers announced the arrivals and departures of other flights and, without anyone noticing anything, the passengers bound for the islands, along with their escorts, ran from one door to another and the guards closed them all. The company lawyers drew up furious demands against the scientists who had caused such disorder, unprecedented in the history of the airport. The guards were unable to contain the tourists and only managed to open and close doors, for the orders to treat foreigners with due consideration had not been rescinded. The tourists brandished their passports and displayed their tickets showing the prices paid for their tours. The duty-free shops closed their doors and barred them from the inside, thinking the long-awaited proletarian uprising had been declared. And the captain of the ship, arms crossed over his chest so that when said revolt exploded, the golden buttons on his jacket wouldn't fly far, awaited the appearance of the lifejackets, while the copilot and the flight attendant came and went without rhyme or reason, colliding with each other and with everyone else, apologizing in all the languages they knew. No one gave them any answers, but only battered them with questions.

Finally, as evening fell, they were able to collect the number of lifejackets necessary for the flight over the sea. New passengers boarded and when the pilot began to warm up the engines with the benzene of his own indignation, the control tower cancelled all flights in view of the bad weather, delaying that trip and all the rest of them, to the passengers' desperation. Then the flight attendant and the *Diomedea irrorata* man trapped the pilot in a corner of the aircraft so that, without undue delay and wrapped in the authority that he said he possessed, he might marry them at once or face the consequences...

The next day, the number of tourists had tripled. The same scenes were repeated, with slight variations, and when the aircraft in question took off at last and felt itself weightless and free in the air, the scientists gave a savage yell of joy. The plane's loudspeakers immediately came on with a laconic welcome aboard, in the pilot's language only, so as to in that fashion slight the Danes who had followed Fritz.

After three hours of pleasant flight, they glimpsed the islands at last. From the air they could be seen emerging serenely from the water in a changing set of every shade of green: blue green, chlorophyll and olive green, sea green, verdigris and dark green, aerugo, greenish-yellow and glaucous green. The sea shone like a jade mirror splashed with the tiny white dots of the waves that appeared and disappeared between the gusts of foam snaking around the sinuous and indolent shorelines.

At last the plane landed in the midst of a solemn and imposing solitude barely interrupted by the howl of the wind. The tourists also maintained an eager silence, interrupted only by the click of their cameras while the wind and the waves left their roar in the stone deafness of the rocks.

His mission completed, the pilot said goodbye to each with a handshake, although he turned his back on the scientists. He hauled off the flight attendant (bathed in tears and kisses) by the ear, but he promised to return on the next flight. The separation of the lovers was terribly sad, but while the captain lifted off with his rescued aircraft and its fifty lifejackets, the tourists placed themselves in an orderly line, trying to capture with their index fingers the first impressions of their eyes on the cellulose negatives, and afterward they climbed into a rattletrap bus that would take them to the pier with a prodigious screeching of brakes along a road that wound through incredible, precipitous chasms above the roaring sea.

At the pier, a launch waited to carry them group by group to another island. The launch, operated by the owners of the Three Chinamen Tavern, came and went industriously until the last trip, when the three expert sailors loaded more cargo than they usually carried and the tired launch, resentful as a Peruvian llama, refused to continue on a horizontal line toward the other island and began to sail on its own account, according to a new, vertical path. Calm and slow, it gave itself over to inertia and sank in the sea—true, only a few meters from shore. Elegant and solemn as the landscape, it ended the last voyage of its life when it felt it was being exploited more than was called for and its fragile wooden structure said, *That's it*, for things rebel sooner than people.

The tourists who knew how to swim, swam. Some of the luggage floated on the tranquil waters, the rest went down with the launch; the fish calmly saw it coming and moved aside. Those who didn't know how to swim were quickly rescued. They gave back the water they had swallowed, they recovered from their fright, they dried off as best they could, looked around to make sure everyone was present, and they prepared to watch the spectacle of the islands, to untangle their mysteries, and to confirm Darwin's theories with their own eyes.

To reach the center of the town, which would be the base for their touristic or scientific activities, they once again divided into groups. The last of them, those from the shipwreck who were soaked to the skin, took longer to leave the pier because Professor Fritz had to examine his voluminous folder page by page until he was sure that not a single letter was missing and he set out a few damp pages to dry in the sun and the wind.

The first passengers had left some time ago. The *Diomedea irrorata* man still had watery eyes and his companions from time to time gave him pats on the back. There was no other vehicle for the stragglers than an old pickup with a wooden cargo box that was used to carry luggage and in which the shipwreck survivors were just barely able to fit.

The pickup began its trip under a good sign, climbing and descending the hills, but when it reached the midpoint, it chose to follow the example of the launch and refused to go a step further. The motor flatly refused to function, tired of going *rr rr rrr* like a lion dying of hunger; rigid and stony, it stopped amid a cloud of dust. The travelers, now accustomed to any pain as if they were the members of a penitential pilgrimage and not the members of a tour group, got down from the truck and with the help of some settlers who seemed to spring from the bushes, pushed the truck up the next slope. The tourists climbed on quickly, like monkeys, and by the time they managed to arrange themselves, the hill came to an end and the pickup stopped just at the start of the next climb; and so, getting down, pushing, climbing up, arranging themselves and once again getting down, pushing, and climbing back in, they reached their destination close to dawn when their other traveling companions, well rested and breakfasted, had suited up in shorts and tennis shoes and were ready for the first crossing in a beautiful yacht that was rocking on the waves.

Part of the delay was due to the fact that the last passengers, whom bad luck took a delight in tormenting, as they believed (though it wasn't that, but rather a maneuver of the bony one to irritate Fritz), spent the night waiting for Cristina. The driver had made a previous commitment. He had to take Cristina to the other side of the island and Cristina didn't arrive. Fritz's threats and protests, and the anguished tourists' pleas were all in vain. The driver couldn't move without Cristina and Cristina was just about to arrive, but Cristina didn't appear before the shadows of night had fallen.

Wrapped up, some against the cold and others out of an uncertainty similar to fear, they prepared to pass the evening. Fritz sat down to think about why things were turning out so complicated for him. It was as if the islands were rejecting his presence and as if the bare-breasted woman had cast him aside, and instead of setting off on foot along a path he knew from memory, he passed the time in dark philosophizing about life and its problems.

They lit a bonfire on the side of the road. The driver—

who was the one who shivered most with cold—began to tell about the apparitions of the baroness and the pirate Morgan which always happened at the edge of midnight.

"Nonsense, superstitions, and foolishness!" Professor Fritz said. "The baroness was never on this island and the pirate Morgan never existed."

He grabbed his folder of notes and without the weight of his backpack, which had gone to the bottom of the sea, set out to make the trip alone and on foot. But when he began to walk and had gone a few meters away from those who remained seated around the fire, he felt that someone was following him. He stopped, looked all around, and found no one. He would have sworn that among the bushes beside the road he had seen the silhouette of a figure that also stopped walking, although its feet seemed not to touch the ground. He started walking again and felt steps behind him. He turned back to look and thought he saw her more clearly. Then there came to him from who knows where a sensation of the unknown, the inexplicable, the undemonstrable to his logic and he felt fear, a fear of being unable to finish the report on the *Opuntia echios*. Terrified, he retraced his steps and felt that she, too, walked in that direction. He sat down beside his companions in misery. Without saying a word, he clutched the folder of papers to his breast and saw that the shadow slipped away out of the glare of the bonfire. He closed his eyes so as to find the precise explanation and when he opened them he saw, as if it were protecting him, another corpulent shadow, one whose eyes had the same glow as the bonfire. He understood then that it was Morgan who even after death continued in open combat with the bony one and tried to prevent her from getting close to Fritz and his papers.

The travelers agreed that they had never in their lives passed such a night, infected with an inexplicable fear, stiff with cold and hunger; they cursed the hour in which it occurred to them to travel to the islands. But as soon as it began to get light, when the dawn began to open a path through the skein of drizzle, the driver yelled excitedly, making everyone forget their fears, "Here comes Cristina!"

The travelers only saw a man arriving with his mule on his back. He didn't come riding her as he should have; instead she rode the weight of her head on his shoulders. Neck against neck, they were the sad image of the horseman carrying his donkey.

"Where's Cristina?"

Everyone looked for her on the road. The driver, stretching, said they would leave in a moment because from where they were to the other end of the island, where they needed to get to, it didn't matter that the truck wouldn't run. It was one long descent down to the beach, an easy slope toward the ocean shore.

They had to make room for Cristina. Grumbling, the passengers arranged themselves in a corner of the pickup. Cristina must be very fat or have a lot of luggage because the driver demanded more and more space.

"Where's Cristina?"

Finally, Cristina climbed up and settled herself, and the battered and sleepy passengers settled themselves in turn between her hooves. Cristina was the mule and she received so much consideration because she was about to give birth.

Immediately, Fritz reconciled himself to all of humanity and to the terrible experience. He sent his thoughts of the night before to the devil and began to live with the throwback, with the sum of two plus two that made five, and the inexplicable whims of the bare-breasted woman, for even she seemed to struggle against boredom and play dirty tricks on her lovers. The protracted wait, the discomforts, the unsettling visions of the night were all worthwhile. Cristina had defeated and demolished the immutable laws of nature. The hybrid had borne fruit. It was an authentic scientific event and Fritz lost his head before it. He measured and palpated Cristina's belly at the risk of losing his balance and falling flat on his face onto the road and he filled his notebook with annotations. He asked every possible question and inspected her owner, who assured him that Cristina was almost human, which was nothing so special given that some humans acted like mules. He confirmed that Cristina had, among other qualities, a great aesthetic sense, and that the pregnancy, just as it did with many spoiled women, had given her the vehement desire to be delivered—he did not say to foal—on a certain island. And he said, full of pride, that he could ignore the wishes of his wife who had already given him seven children, but that he could not ignore the wishes of Cristina, who was going to be a mother for the first time. So the baby would be born on the most beautiful island in the world, the one that was covered all over with red *muyuyos* as if it had been carpeted, that island of white rocks that looked like marble or stones covered with a layer of mother-of-pearl that, in fact, was nothing but the excrement of the seagulls and the frigate birds on the impassive rock. There, atop the red carpet and the shine of the marble, between the murmur of the sea and the bellowing of the seals, Cristina would give birth, the only mule ever to become a mother.

From that moment on, Fritz didn't leave Cristina for an instant. He momentarily forgot about his *Opuntia echios* and concentrated all of his capacity for work on making every possible note and annotation about the gestation and the delivery until the day on which Cristina realized her dream and gave birth to a beautiful little white mule. Her owner was happy with the event and insisted on baptizing him with the name Felipe II, in honor of Prince Philip of England who had been in the islands some months earlier, but although Fritz was the godfather, and did his utmost to explain that the name didn't suit the little mule because he was white and beautiful, and so perhaps he could be Felipe the Handsome, but never Felipe II, who was entirely the opposite... but the owner was more stubborn than Cristina.

Then Fritz began to pay attention to his specific mission,

namely the *Opuntia echios*. He dedicated himself to them and when he was in the best part of his research, which was his reason for living, one gray morning on which the sun, with a premonition of catastrophe, refused to come out, he heard a series of shots that tore the air and shredded the tranquility of the islands. The bony one who lived in the barracks of the military zone was having a birthday and had begun to celebrate.

The good people asked themselves who could be shooting that way, interrupting the long siesta of the tortoises, the voracious appetite of the slow cormorants, the mating dances of the albatross, the pecking of the round finches, the bellow of the shiny seals, the stealthy creep of the centipedes, the movement of the fish in the crystalline waters, the slither of the black iguanas, and the growth of the white, red, and black corals?

The question hung in the air before another burst of gunfire. Overawed with surprise, the islanders didn't know what to do or what to say. A few hours later, they learned the truth. A fishing boat unloaded the horrible news wrapped up with the nets and the fishing tackle: the soldiers of the zone had been taking target practice against the islands' animals.*

The bony one was trying to calm the gale of her anxieties. She would always be alone. Although she was a woman, she would never manage to beget a child. A normal

---

* An event that occurred under the military Junta in 1963. [trans. note: footnote in the original.]

119

man would never fall in love with her. Only the desperate claimed her and although she was capable of loving with the most tender, most intelligent, most intuitive, and most sincere love, she would always be alone. For that reason, from time to time she was wicked.

When Fritz heard the news, he trembled with indignation, he thought of the bare-breasted woman and his eyes filled with tears at his inability to fight against barbarism. An organic shudder shook his organism in spasms and death rattles and his flesh opened painlessly. At once a pair of sturdy wings covered with gray feathers sprouted from his shoulder blades. He saw the silhouette of the woman who had tried to approach him when they were around the bonfire and he knew who she was. When Fritz felt his wings, he understood that he had an urgent mission and he took flight.

Only seven pink flamingoes remained on Floreana Island. The soldiers crouched in the thickets and waited for them to reappear so as to continue their stupid task. Fritz flew to them and sent them to hide themselves in the hollows of the rocks; the slender flamingoes, the color of coral, disappeared like smoke. He flew to Isabella Island and alerted the albatross. He flew to Fernandina and informed the penguins. From island to island he went, spreading the news that a bunch of depraved men had gone crazy, but when he returned to Santa Cruz, his flight missed by a few particles of a second; the bony one was embracing the soldiers who were aiming at Felipe II and when Fritz tried to tell him to run and hide himself, together, godfather and godson shared the shots between them and embarked on their journey along the same path taken by Morgan when he was transformed into a butterfly, through the same air into which the shrunken Alirio disappeared, along the same oblique ray of sunlight Iridia climbed.

Felipe II allowed Fritz to ride him. The pallid one tried to climb up on his rump, but Felipe II gave her a kick to the sacrum. The mule and the horseman disappeared in the salt air of the islands. The children at the Genoveva de Brabante School managed to see them and shouted: "Look, look at that comet, we've never seen one so large and so bright!"

Estenia

The illusions in Estenia's mind were like the multiple and multicolored images of a chameleon inside a kaleidoscope until one day, diving among them, she found them vacuous and small for her height, which had begun to increase after she turned twenty. She put them aside and set herself to reading Greek mythology, where she came across the myth of Prometheus. Her life changed forever when she learned that the god had modeled the body of the first man out of clay, that he had softened the clay with his own tears to make it in his likeness, that because of those tears humanity had been born with its back to happiness. Then the god, feeling sorry for and hurting for his imperfect creation, stole the sacred fire from Vulcan and gave it to men, but thundering Jupiter punished his audacity, condemning him to live chained to the solitary rocks where the vultures devoured his entrails that then renewed themselves each day, as if the liver, the heart, and the kidneys had immortal roots.

It was then that Estenia, moved, closed the book of mythology. From that very instant, she felt the call of a latent vocation that was like the tolling of a great bell in her ears. That *bong! bong!* from the heights made her break off with her fiancé and with the rest of her illusions. She consecrated herself to teaching as if she were a vestal virgin, turning her life completely around, retracing her steps up to that point and asking herself insistently what her mother could have been thinking when she baptized her with the bland name of Estenia in place of Promethea.

She felt the god's own arrogance, isolated in her mission and chained to her destiny of carrying light to mankind and, as she looked at the waters of the Pontus Euxinus she understood that she could not be a shared woman because she could not think of living in any other way, or loving other loves, despite having a heart too big for her small size.

When she became a teacher she began to imagine that all children's minds were like unlit candles and that her mission should be to light them with the spark of knowledge that she had not stolen from any god, but which she had acquired so as to give it to the schoolchildren because she was predestined to banish the shadows of ignorance, which since the time of Prometheus had chained suffering humanity; and this mission could not be shared with another because, instead of having children of her own, she could well be the true mother of all the children of the islands. She thought that although the home was a highly serious and responsible institution, she could not be circumscribed by four walls and a husband until times changed and the housewife was considered in a different way than was habitual, because when—and high time— slaves had disappeared, housework had remained as the continuation of slavery and it shouldn't be that way. That work of degrading origin had to be cleansed of its opprobrious past, vindicated, placed in a different category of values. Professional motherhood should be created. Up until now, motherhood had been based only in the instinct to preserve the species, and although such motherhood might continue taking care of cleanings and kitchens, it also had to make up or at least complete the work of the elementary school, the high school, the university, and then provide advice and assistance in the job and in the profession of the man whom she might choose as companion; but as things weren't as Estenia thought they should be, she would have to complete from her own school what mothers alone, supported only by their instincts, could not do.

The most memorable day of her life was when she

received her appointment as teacher in the far off islands.
She went crazy with happiness and immediately prepared
her luggage, which consisted of many books battered with
use, a little summer clothing, some insipid primers, some
colored pencils, a pile of notebooks, a framed image of
the tricolor flag and the national seal, a very long pointer
which was to point out on the map the borders of the
country which in the old days was enormous, but no longer
was—even so, the students had to keep pointing it out,
standing on tiptoes and reciting with a hint of sadness that
in the mountainous North it reached up to Pasto, Buga,
Chanepanchica and Guarchicona, and that to the South it
stretched beyond Piura. To show that, the pointer was no
longer necessary; instead the student had to squat down on
all fours, crawling on the floor, tracing with an index finger
and with the nostalgia of one who searches for something
lost, the line of the old borders, and then straightening up
little by little, to say that we lost the Amazon River... And
the pointer also served to hit misbehaving children and
those who couldn't or wouldn't repeat what their teachers
taught. She carried a box of white chalk and another
of colored chalk, and erasers and rulers and cardboard
and compasses to make the compass rose, and a decree
from the Government signed with a hundred flourishes
authorizing the establishment of a school which would be
called Genoveva Benavides, which was the sacred name
of the mother of the President General who extended his
surname and the power of his family to the island latitudes

and which among other things said that the school was being created because *you have only one mother.*

But when Estenia arrived in the islands, after eight days of sailing and sailing, the telegraph's gossip arrived ahead of her to say that the President General was no longer such. And it was then that Estenia, faithful to her principles, sensibly transformed, with the help of her wits and an ink eraser, Genoveva Benavides into Genoveva de Brabante which was better known and more beloved by the children of any school and although Mrs. Benavides sent her a Christmas check from time to time, that was forever the name of the school.

One day, when everything was proceeding in the best fashion thanks to the fact that Miss Estenia multiplied herself across the six grades of the school, the recess hour ended and the children didn't want to go back into class because they could see in the distance the silhouette of the *Floreana.* Estenia extended recess and ran down to the beach. She waited impatiently for her usual packet of out-dated newspapers, she looked through them as eagerly as ever and she read the most important of the news items. She swallowed hard, ran back up to the school and brandishing the bell, *ding ding ding ding*, she didn't stop ringing it until all of the island's inhabitants were on the school patio. Then she stood on a chair and with great emotion spread the news to the winds:

"A princess, Princess Anne, Princess Anne of England herself, is going to come to these islands on a honeymoon trip! She'll come to visit us, imagine it, she'll be here very soon!"

The news caused the commotion of a tidal wave. A princess isn't the same as a prince, Miss Estenia assured her astonished listeners. Prince Philip, father of Princess Anne and namesake of Cristina's son, had had the poor taste to arrive in the islands a few years earlier in slacks and shirtsleeves as if he were any other mortal and not who he was. He hadn't worn a mantle or a crown and he arrived incognito, who knows from what motives, that's how insipid the English are. But Princess Anne would be different because she was coming on her honeymoon and she was a princess. She would arrive as a real queen should arrive, with the prince consort at her side or, more accurately, a little behind, as the rules of etiquette prescribed, because in such matters the English were very severe, they weren't like the North American hippies who overran the islands, chewing gum, putting their feet on the tables at the Three Chinamen bar, smoking marihuana and giving a bad example to the children of the school, the work of her own hands to whom she had dedicated her life doing what Prometheus had done.

When she finished speaking, at that very instant, she got to work. She sat down at her table and wrote various communiqués to the parents of her students and to the island authorities, exhorting them to meet that evening on the school patio. She suspended classes and with her usual diligence, she set out resolutely on the path to the house of

San Pío Pascual and Santa Livina to share the news, hand them the communiqué and ask them to collaborate. She climbed up the hill and when she arrived, she sat down out of breath in the same chair where Morgan would have sat. Santa Livina ran to prepare the lemonade so as to have an excuse to be present in case this was another confession, and when she heard them arguing heatedly and not talking quietly as she had expected, she hid the drink.

San Pío Pascual could not clearly see the role that the reception committee was supposed to play and therefore he refused to participate, adducing, among other reasons, the fact that the non-celibate pastors who might father children and the Catholic priests in cassocks like the one he wore, had not even given each other the time of day since the time of Henry VIII, and that since Princess Anne belonged to them and not to him, he did not want any dealings with her or hers, and that he would make no demonstration, not even one of courtesy, because he didn't want to, nor did he care about people who came to the islands bringing pernicious customs, and he said it was the most ridiculous thing he'd ever heard when she proposed to ring the bells of the church that was not yet built, and he was very sorry not to be able to make her happy, but though she asked him on her knees he would not give a single peal, no matter who disembarked, because if he were to start paying attention to her, then he would cease to be a priest and would instead become the bell-ringer for all the people who arrived. And he told her that the bells of the church that was not yet built (due to the laziness of the residents) had specific missions to carry out, such as calling the faithful—who every day were less assiduous—to religious services, and not any other thing of such a worldly cast as ringing out the arrival of a princess who wasn't even Catholic.

From the bamboo rocker, with the rhythmic movement and the sound of dry wood, *sss sss sss*, Santa Livina approved all of San Pío Pascual's words. She was dying to intervene in the conversation.

Estenia, red with indignation at the refusal and because the sermon was so long, flung in her turn the words fatherland, patriotism, international prestige, and other related terms with which she seemed to shake the front of his cassock: "Sermons for *me!*"

But he remained stony as a rock. Estenia brandished the argument that Princess Anne had no reason to be Protestant, that she must be a Catholic like her mother, because she well remembered she had been married in a cathedral, Estenia didn't remember the name of it, but it was gothic, gothic which is the style of the folded hands.

Santa Livina interrupted, dragging the rocking chair as if it were made of straw into the very center of the discussion: "Do you not know, you who call yourself a teacher, that in that nation of heretics, the Catholic cathedrals alternate, in spiritual concubinage, with Protestant cathedrals?"

Estenia was left speechless, not because of what she heard, but because it was two against one. Santa Livina took advantage of her lapse, she rolled up her sleeves and did what she had always wanted to do, which was to emulate San Pío Pascual in his sermons: "And even if it were not so, England is the country with the highest divorce rate in the world. That country is not the realm of any Elizabeth but the kingdom of pornography. Have not you heard Tom Jones' songs? Lust and more lust. And that tired old Queen Elizabeth, knowest thou what she did one fine day?"

San Pío Pascual, surprised by the vigor of her words, watched Estenia, interrogating her with his eyes to find out if she knew what Elizabeth had done, and Estenia looked back at him open-mouthed at the unheard of use of such antiquated and pretentious grammar, in the face of which silence, Santa Livina continued triumphantly:

"Dost thou not know? Well, then. She had the nerve to decorate, right in the middle of Parliament, a mob of indecent, drug-addicted, faggot singers, to mention only the least of it. She decorated the Beatles! Emblems of corruption and sin. Elizabeth did that, and ye wouldst give her daughter the royal welcome?"

"Not I, not I," responded San Pío Pascual, offended.

Estenia could not get past her astonishment and she let Santa Livina continue, hearing her say, as if in a dream, that no one could take issue with her about anything, because she was the only person in the islands who received, monthly, real information from Catholic magazines and not cheap broadsheets; that she was well informed and she knew all about the horrors that were taking place in the corrupted world.

"And no matter how much I ponder it, I cannot explain to myself, what God of the Sacred Heavens is doing that he does not send the fires of Sodom and Gomorrah against ye, the impious. What is happening, that it does not rain fire?"

Estenia finally managed to recover, and she was beside herself, because she did not tolerate anyone, least of all Santa Livina, putting on intellectual airs in her presence after what had happened with Alirio who had published more than a dozen books and was extremely well known in the world of letters, but when it came right down to it was incapable of giving even a bad class to the school's first graders, let alone delivering a lecture, don't even mention speaking by radio to the islands' inhabitants in a coherent fashion, as happened with the much discussed program he had, and so it was clear that she, along with the Parents' Committee had been behind the bomb.

Estenia swallowed hard and, placing herself in front of Santa Livina, she spat at her, saying that was not the way to speak in the present day, that they had even invented the word ecumenism which—if she'd pardon the rhyme—meant "we're all the same-ism".

San Pío Pascual, upon realizing that Estenia was stepping onto his home turf, did not let her continue, and snatching the word from her he told her that things were as they were due to things similar to that self-same ecumenism, for that was what produced schisms and confusions, and the worst was that anyone and everyone believed themselves authorized to speak about any topic, and that she should not say a single word more about the matter, because he and his aunt boasted of being, and would remain unto death, authentic Catholics, apostolic and Roman.

Estenia interrupted him, saying, "Not a bit Roman, ladies and gentlemen, because everyone knows you were born in Pujilí, not in Italy."

Santa Livina flew off the handle, she forgot about the tone of the sermon and the difficult *thou* tense, but she didn't get into it with Estenia who was now standing threateningly; instead she lit into the royal family that was far away and, being as cowardly as a rat, she said of one who couldn't defend herself that Princess Anne was of the same ilk as her Aunt Margaret who was causing scandal after scandal in the European courts, and spent her life squandering the income of the kingdom in lewd activities, and was a divorcee, and had innumerable lovers, and that in the same newspaper which Estenia had brought there was a photo of the aunt who was not the image of what a princess of royal blood should be, but rather of a whore like Iridia who had come to corrupt the men of the islands.

"Because with that neckline—imagine! That's not even suitable for these parts where the heat is killing us, still less a country where it snows. This photo is the limit! You can see practically everything!"

San Pío Pascual asked for the newspaper so as to see what you could see, and Santa Livina folded it in one swipe and sat down on top of it so that no one could see anything.

Estenia was like an infuriated wave and said she was leaving. She went away without saying goodbye, walking tall, shaking her head and muttering under her breath, "With this class of people, there can be no progress."

As the evening fell, however, the meeting that had been agreed upon was celebrated without the religious authorities, who after all had only the bell for the church that had not yet been built. The session produced great results: a celebrations committee was named and a permanent secretary for the minutes. It was the first time bureaucracy set up camp in the islands. Immediately, vibrant with the enthusiasm that Miss Estenia knew how to communicate, they began to organize themselves under the supervision of:

MADAM PRESIDENT OF THE CENTRAL COMMITTEE:
Miss Lady Professor Estenia León
HONORARY PRESIDENT OF THE RECEPTION COMMITTEE:
The Honorable Mr. Storekeeper Nicasio Jeria

&

PERMANENT SECRETARY OF THE MINUTES:
The Honorable Mr. Farmer Etilenio Chérrez.

That same night Estenia, still furious with San Pío Pascual and Santa Livina, set about the task of investigating the colors of the English flag. She spent hours and hours looking laboriously through all of the available books until she discovered that England and Great Britain were parts of the same island and were so fused together that it was not possible to tell which was the northern part and which the southern. She deduced that some Englishmen could be Greatbritanian but not all Greatbritanians turned out to be English; nevertheless, the capital of the United Kingdom— as it was also called—was still London, which had its famous Tower, its foggy climate, and its River Thames.

The next day she woke up calmer and more lucid. As soon as she jumped out of bed, she shouted as if to make sure her voice would reach the house of San Pío Pascual and Santa Livina, who lived far away, "Always look on the bright side!"

But time was bearing down on her and the members of the committee couldn't send to the mainland for the quantity of fabric necessary to make the outfits for the schoolchildren who were to form the Honor Guard in the colors of the Greatbritanian flag. Estenia solved the problem by sacrificing, patriotically and selflessly, two sets of sheets from her very own virginal bed.

Over several days, she soaked the sheets in blue water, collecting the little balls for bluing clothes that the women had stored but, since the sheets wouldn't take on the blue shown in the geography book, and since she had only a vague idea of how her grandmother used to prepare the methylene blue soap, she dumped half a liter of the precious medicine into the pots where the fabric was boiling, to the despair of the pharmacist who knew that he would be left without clients when a plague of sore throats struck and they went en masse to line up at the door to Brigita's house to be cured with her herbs and potions.

The sheets finally ended up between faded and stained, between blue and bluish, between overseas blue and ultramarine blue, between deep blue and indigo, between indigo and sapphire, between azure and sky blue, like the watercolor of ocean and sky made by a disabled child, with storms and thunderheads at every turn.

"Her Majesty will excuse our poverty," Estenia said, put out. "Things aren't valuable in and of themselves, but for the intention we bring to them."

The days began to have thirty hours. Armed with a pair of scissors, Estenia worked marvels with the sheets. She made twelve simple little tunics, since the children who would wear them were scrawny. She crossed and recrossed them with strips of blue and red crepe paper, and after spreading and stretching the fabric, wrinkling and unwrinkling the paper streamers, basting and then unbasting the necklines and armholes, putting a safety pin here and some straight pins there, the uniforms for the princess's Honor Guard were ready. Estenia had lifted all of the island's inhabitants out of the easy chair of boredom. Those were absurd, crazy days. Princess Anne's arrival, even the princess herself, was nothing compared to the passion they put into what they were doing. They lived with such intensity that for a long time they retained a sense that there had been but a single, solitary family in the islands and that Estenia was the mother, with a motherhood that had evolved beyond biological motherhood.

When they finished making the uniforms, the children spent long hours rehearsing the bow of high etiquette or protocol, as Miss Estenia explained it, which consisted in bending forward, bending the right leg a bit to the outside, stretching the left leg back and making a gesture with the right hand as if one were scattering rose petals over a supposed carpet, at the same time keeping the forehead high and the left hand extended, and they should smile at the members of the royal court. Estenia beat the air with her ever-present pointer and kept the rhythm:

"Step forward, flex, *one, two*; flex, *one, two*; smile, left arm forward, *one, two*; right arm, *one, two*. Smile, *one, two*."

During the rehearsals, the shopkeeper Jeria, who didn't miss a thing, very sensibly suggested to the teacher that the students would do it better if instead of telling them they should make a gesture as if to throw rose petals, they should tell them to make the gesture of throwing corn to the hens, a suggestion that was carried out and gave excellent results, because the children understood instantly what that meant and made the appropriate movement.

"Step forward, *one, two*; flex, *one, two*; flex, *one, two*; smile, *one, two*; corn, *one, two*. Smile *one, two*."

For his part, Jeria, who was the richest man in the islands and was undertaking all the expenses (on the condition that he would be the first to kiss the perfumed hand of Princess Anne) didn't want to be left behind by the zeal of Estenia—with her the sacrifice of two sets of sheets—and he put his three wives into the only motorboat there was and sent them to the main island with urgent orders to have three dresses made, one yellow, one blue, and one red. They should represent the fatherland in a trio of colors. He ordered them to return on the eve of the great day, made up and with their hair done by the woman who called herself not a simple hairdresser, but the only stylist in the islands. The three obeyed without complaint and they had no choice but to leave, but they went in an ill humor, resentful of the imperative to live with each other and because they would not be present for the preparations, but when the boat was on the high seas, little by little they became excited about the role they would play upon their return and also because they began to think about long, low-cut dresses, very elegant, which had been discussed and selected by the members of the Committee, taking into account—in the distribution of colors—the generosity or stinginess of the flesh of each; given that she who would wear yellow was heavier and taller than the other two, the matter of the colors of the national flag was made perfectly clear. In addition, the three would be the ones to give Princess Anne a bouquet of flowers decorated with snails and cockleshells from the shore. At dawn on the great day, Jeria's children—who were many, since they were born in triplicate—would go to the higher elevations in search of wild orchids.

Half the town showed up to wave goodbye to the three women who sat in the motor launch trying to maintain their distance and underscore their rivalry. The one who was going to wear yellow sat down facing the other two, opened a parasol, and put one tremendous thigh over the other so that the two could see the quantity and the quality of her flesh. The one who would wear blue, who was the youngest and most spoiled because of being the most recently acquired, began to flirt shamelessly with the owner of the boat, so as to demonstrate to the others her wit and resources. And the one who was going to wear red, who was the oldest and felt she had the most rights, did not say a single word during the whole trip but rather splashed the others with grimaces of disdain and signs that something nearby smelled bad. Saying goodbye to them on the pier, Jeria was very worried and reminded them nonstop to behave well and not fight, they should look on one another as sisters, at least for a few days, they must keep in mind the high mission that the Committee had entrusted to them and not make him look bad in front of the inhabitants of the other island.

At night, Estenia worked feverishly on the preparation of the welcome speech, lamenting constantly the disappearance of Alirio, who had seen his name in print in books, newspapers, and magazines and who now could give her no help in such a difficult situation. The speech, handwritten in perfect letters in green ink, took up eight sheets of paper, making reference in those pages to King Arthur and the Knights of the Round Table, to Saint George and his dragon, to the pirate Drake and his incursions into the islands and the ports of the mainland, to Sir Winston Churchill and his resemblance to all of the babies in the world, to Anne Boleyn and her palace scandals, to John Lackland and to other great personages who filled the yellowing pages of an old Bristol almanac that the pharmacist found when he was looking among the empty bottles for a substitute for methylene blue.

The streets were swept and sprinkled. Twenty triumphal arches were placed at the spots that Princess Anne and her retinue would pass, decorated with streamers and Chinese lanterns made by the schoolchildren. A detachment from the military base practiced a well-tuned National Anthem, and since no one knew the notes to the Greatbritanian anthem, they practiced in its place various marches that would be played before and after the disembarkation. Estenia had a fit of rage when the band director wanted to include in the repertoire the notes of *El Chulla Quiteño*. Estenia argued that her Highness had no reason to know about *chullas* or Quiteños either.

Brigita would prepare ten pitchers of lemonade and of other juices from fruits grown in her orchard and irrigated with the water that had mysteriously appeared the same day Alirio disappeared—though he, nevertheless, was sometimes seen talking with Iridia. Richardson had promised to make a special bread and also cookies in the shape of tortoises, iguanas, seals, albatross, finches, all crunchy and covered with sesame seeds.

Everyone had caught Estenia's enthusiasm, and the

great day finally arrived, that being, as the newspaper put it, the twentieth of December of the current year.

At the last minute, San Pío Pascual and Santa Livina, hurt by the bitter scowls of their neighbors and the way they pretended they didn't exist, made peace with them and with Miss Estenia, and they offered to personally ring the bells of the church that had not yet been built. They would, granted, give the bell forty good solid peals, but not one more, while the boat anchored and the princess with all her retinue disembarked.

At seven o'clock sharp all of the island's inhabitants were up. The schoolchildren, dressed as Greatbritanians, protected their Honor Guard uniforms from the persistent drizzle by covering themselves with sheets of newsprint. A few outfits began to fade and fall apart in the comings and goings, well sprinkled with pinches from Miss Estenia who, learning the speech by heart, had slept only a few hours and who never took her eyes off the horizon and made little hops of impatience on the improvised pier, cursing the pain and fatigue caused by the extremely high heeled shoes which she hadn't worn in years and the tight dress that obliged her to remain upright, fearing every minute that the seams might explode and out would stampede the kilos of tranquility that she had accumulated during her stay in the islands.

Jeria's three wives had arrived that same day at four in the morning, just as planned, punctual and tired, stoically bearing the discomforts and the squabbling of the forced and unbearable coexistence of a diminished, leaderless harem on a four day voyage. They had spent the night awake, seated nicely to starboard, worse for wear and aching, but upright and curled, each with a little net to protect her ringlets from the mischievous ocean breeze— for not a single hair should move within the elaborate curlicues, snails, and cockleshells of the hairdresser that had cost the father of their respective children so much money—and with the packet of the new dress, still fresh from the basting, folded over the respective knees of each one and protected in plastic bags from the salt drops of the immense sea.

The three-time husband waited uneasily, and when they told him the launch was arriving, he leapt out of the desolate, oh-so-sad bed of the obligatory bachelor, took a lantern, and went down to the dock to wait. He lit them up one by one and gave his approval of the complicated hairstyles. The three women didn't even have the energy to harass him with their gossip and complaints. They dozed another hour, and when the sun came out and lit up their wilted faces and the six circles under their eyes, they began to spruce themselves up as best they could, they put on the low-cut dresses and in patriotic single file, they went to occupy the spots that Miss Estenia had assigned. The first, who was the largest and fattest and who was dressed in yellow, got herself into a girdle with the aid of her neighbors. The second, who was dressed in blue and who was the most sesquipedalian and also spoiled because of being the youngest and most recently acquired, covered herself with jewels and wristwatches. The third, who was the one of longest standing and was dressed in red, walked like a sleepwalker and was dying to send everything to the devil. They were served large cups of black coffee so that they would stop yawning and wouldn't fall asleep in the course of the long ceremony. Holding a huge bouquet of wild orchids in which the morning dew still twinkled, they placed themselves after the children who formed the Honor Guard and felt somewhat compensated for the hardships they had experienced when they saw the envious looks of the other women, who didn't belong to Jeria.

Estenia, very nervous, watched over all of the details and kept pinching the children who wouldn't stand still. She folded and unfolded the paper with the speech that she knew from memory and even acted out in the parts with the greatest Greatbritanian content. She pointed out the spot that corresponded to each person present and she even interfered with the soldiers and their respective musical instruments, because it did not please her that the members of the military band stood at ease, rather than at attention like the little figures in black pants and red jackets, with their gold epaulettes and matching buttons and the wasps' nest of a black cap on their heads that were drawn in the geography book to illustrate the pages corresponding to Great Britain. And the real soldiers, who in no way resembled those little figures, weren't sure if they should obey her or their captain, who also didn't know if he gave the orders to his band or if it was Miss Estenia who affected the bearing of a general and had taken command of the island, sometimes watching the empty horizon and sometimes watching the post where the bell from the church that had not yet been built was hung so as to confirm and reconfirm that San Pío Pascual and Santa Livina remained in their spots with the cord of the bell clapper in hand, ready to begin the peals as they had agreed to do after their big fight.

Estenia wasn't still even for a second. She tried the lemonade Brigita had made to see if it was cold and up to the level of a royal palate. She touched the cookies freshly baked by Richardson—shaped like birds, reptiles, and mammals—that were piled up on various trays. She arranged and stretched the pleats of a piece of damask that Jeria had loaned to cover the age and the faded spots on a wicker armchair that, in spite of everything, looked like a real throne.

Richardson was happy, enchanted with the colorful atmosphere and the party mood. And the people, the good people of the islands, crowded onto the pier maintaining a respectful silence and a court composure, conscious of being the protagonists in a national event, as if from one moment to the next her Serene Majesty were about to appear; they remained standing, without breakfast, with expressions befitting the circumstances, in their best Sunday clothes, starched and ironed, waiting eagerly.

And eight o'clock came, and nine, and then twelve

and no one moved from the spot even to go have lunch, and besides, it had not occurred to anyone to cook that day, since they were afraid of missing the spectacle of a real princess landing, stepping off an immense ship to the sound of bugles and trumpets in a gown embroidered with precious stones, a great mantle of velvet edged in ermine, the kilometer-long train borne by little blond pages, wearing on her head a crown of diamonds and sapphires, and carrying a golden scepter that must be the same as the magic wand of Cinderella's fairy godmother.

And the sun came out earlier than on other days, because it didn't want to miss the spectacle either. It bore down and squeezed their shoulders and unmoving heads, and the children, under the penetrating gaze of Estenia, began to try to take off their bluish tunics crossed with blue and red crepe paper, and to line up in front of her asking permission to go to the school bathroom every five minutes.

And Jeria's three wives, who had reached the limit of their endurance, began to elbow each other and give each other nasty looks, tired and fed up with the tripartite holding of the wild orchid bouquet of which nothing remained but a heap of wilted and sticky petals. And the one in blue, who was the most sesquipedalian and spoiled by their husband, committed the first offence, giving the one in yellow, who was the biggest and fattest—like half the national flag—a sneaky, strong stamp, and that one dug her sharp nails into this one's arm, and when Jeria was distracted, his gaze lost on the horizon, trying to be the first to make out the ship that would arrive any moment, the one in blue pulled out all at once the hairpins that held up the chignon of the one in red, because the one in red's hand cramped up so she stopped holding up the bouquet of orchids which the one in yellow had also stopped holding and when the one in blue realized that she was the only one holding the bouquet, she threw it on the ground. Then the one in red's hair all fell down, tangled and limp, and when the one in yellow was about to throw herself on the traitor and smother her with her weight because the one in red was busy looking for her hairpins, Jeria came running back from the horizon, and as he, too, was nervous and upset because of the long wait, he restrained the urge to slap all three, and he only threatened them, saying that if they didn't keep still and be quiet and behave like ladies, he would take off his leather belt with the silver buckle and give them a good trashing in front of the whole crowd. And the three women turned red with embarrassment because everyone was looking at them and talking about what had happened. They bowed their heads and held back tears. And Estenia rushed over at a bound, she gathered up the scattered bouquet, and when she saw the calamity that had befallen them she, too, held back tears.

And the good people, downcast and saddened, began to back up very slowly toward their houses, taking advantage of any lapse of Miss Estenia's attention. And three o'clock came, and four, and five, and close to six in the evening, the sun, which was also sad and tired, took off the gala rays it had donned for that day and sank into the sea, giving itself a dip of color. And seven o'clock came, and eight, and nine, and the ship with her Serene Majesty never arrived.

And at ten, Estenia went home. She took off the extremely high-heeled shoes that had tortured her all day, she took off the tight dress, and she gave free rein to her flesh and to her tears, crying inconsolably; she cried until eleven and at twelve she fell asleep out of pure fatigue and sadness and she dreamt that Princess Anne arrived in the islands, dressed just as she had imagined her, and after the welcome speech that was applauded at length by all of those present, Princess Anne, moved, took off the diamond ring that she always wore on her ring finger and she transferred it to Estenia's ring finger, sealing a pact of friendship, and afterward she gave her a kiss of thanks on the cheek, and there was no fiasco and no sadness among the people who had put their entire souls into preparing the event.

A few more months passed, and the *Floreana* anchored once again, and Estenia again received her customary pile of battered newspapers, and as she was leafing through the outdated pages, she saw a photograph that left her stunned and breathless: Princess Anne had disembarked on the island on the scheduled day and had passed under the noses of the inhabitants who were busy with preparations, but no one had paid her any heed or even noticed her because she arrived on a common, everyday yacht and because she wore blue jeans, a checked shirt, and tennis shoes.

Santa Livina was right when she said the world was

rotten and that the end of ends was approaching. Estenia could not overcome her astonishment. "An authentic princess, of royal blood and from such an important country, dressed like any other vulgar tourist!"

Estentia continued to dream, persistently, the same dream. She began to go to bed earlier so as to better see all the details of the great day, until she had not the least doubt that in reality Princess Anne had arrived at the island in her palatial ship and had listened to Estenia's speech, had stroked the heads of the children who formed the Honor Guard, drunk Brigita's lemonade—because she was very thirsty—and eaten the cookies made by the gringo Richardson, accepted the huge bouquet of orchids that Jeria's three wives presented to her, and she had sat down on the great throne covered with the piece of damask. And that was when Miss Estenia turned the house upside down hunting desperately for the diamond ring that the princess had given her, and when she arrived at school late, telling everyone there were thieves on the island, she began her classes by asking the children: "Do you remember the great day when Princess Anne arrived in a white ship that didn't look like a ship but rather a floating castle, and she disembarked to the tune of the national anthem, and said that the Genoveva de Brabante School was the best school out of all those she had visited? And do you remember the dress studded with pearls and diamonds and the ermine mantle that she wore?"

The schoolchildren squirmed uneasily, remembering

only the long wait under the burning sun and the pinches of that horrible day, and it began to seem to them that Miss Estenia—who never made a mistake—was pronouncing the words badly, but they didn't dare contradict her. They had never before heard the word ermine, but rather aluminum, the aluminum of the pots their mothers cooked in, the aluminum of the bucket in which they carried the milk, the aluminum of the jug in which the coffee was made, and they kept remembering the long wait and the fatigue, the heat and the long faces of the people. But Miss Estenia kept repeating that the princess's crown glinted in the sunlight, and that there was a star on the tip of her scepter, and since the gaping children still looked doubtful, Estenia, who had become a big fan of those pinches, treated the most reluctant to four or five, until everyone began to see how in fact Princess Anne walked down the street by the school with her royal entourage every few minutes.

After the arrival of Princess Anne, who made herself an ordinary person on the islands, normal life resumed its hot, monotonous course. Estenia kept looking for her lost ring in every corner of the house and she kept lighting little candles in the children's minds to banish the shadows of ignorance. Princess Anne had not been able to put aside Prometheus. When every mind was without shadows, because the children had learned to read and to write and they knew by memory the borders of the nation of today and of yesterday, and many other things about mathematics and spelling, and the names of the highest mountains and the names of the heroes of the nation, Estenia began to grow desperate, this time for real and with good reason.

A moment arrived in which there were no children to teach nor candles to light. Every day there were fewer births and although the people got married, as a few would have it; or started living in sin, according to San Pío Pascual and Santa Livina; they cuddled up, according to the owner of the Hotel Florida, who was a Spaniard; they pulled the covers up, according to Manuel Yuquilema who waited tables at the hotel; they shacked up, they made do, they fooled around—nothing had any result. Brigita had her waiting room full and the famous prescription for lettuce soup with catfish head and the infusion of *guayusa* leaves on an empty stomach, and the infusions of fig leaves on work days, and the wife's lashing of the husband in the middle of a field planted to squash, had no effect, which was really inconceivable, because Brigita could make the stones fertile and her prescriptions had never failed, not even with menopausal old women.

The longed-for children were not born and the Genoveva de Brabante School shrunk little by little. There was no longer a first grade, or a second, or a third. The women anxiously prodded their empty wombs and the men their erect and useless members. They knew that the bony one was staying at the barracks, but it was evident that she was making use of someone else as well to get in the way of life.

Estenia tried to determine what curse had weighed on

the island in recent years. Ever since the arrival of Alirio, there had been no more children. Iridia had gone to all kinds of effort and she left without conceiving the green-eyed child she hoped for. When the scientists arrived, the first grade was closed. San Pío Pascual and Santa Livina remembered having celebrated only two baptisms of already grown children and those had clear, feline eyes that testified, if not to the paternity, at least to the grandpaternity of Morgan, as if only the people of his blood were free of the curse.

When the last seven children to be born in the islands reached the sixth grade, Estenia arrived at a paroxysm. The Genoveva de Brabante School would close its doors, and she pondered and investigated until it became clear that the one person responsible was the foreigner Richardson who had arrived in the islands to establish the Hot Cakes Bakery exactly eleven years, nine months, and a few days earlier. What would become of her and of her life when the school closed...? To whom would she carry the spark of knowledge...? What would become of her and of her former students amidst the shadows of ignorance...? What would become of their royal highnesses when they disembarked on the islands and found themselves without honor guard and without anyone to give them even a diminished welcome speech...? Whom would she teach to recite the lines of the poet Alirio, made famous by his disappearance...? To whom would she explain what an adjective was, and a rectangle...? To whom would she talk about vertebrates and national heroes...?

The last day that the last child left the school to go to the mainland, Estenia said goodbye, reduced to a sea of tears. She padlocked the school doors, went home, and looked for a candle; she lit the candle and began to walk. She carried the flame in spite of the fact that the sun shone as never before. She was resolute and determined, her hair loose and her head held high. She carried the spark of knowledge in one hand and with the other she made a screen so that the wind would not extinguish it. She knew that the bony one could start a fire, but she could not put her claw into the flame. The bony one wanted Estenia and her candle, and when she got close and tried to blow it out with her fetid breath, Estenia began to run, but the pallid one touched her on the shoulder.

Estenia stopped running. The candle was guttering and so she walked and walked, convinced that she was walking in a straight line, but as that was not possible, being on an island, she circled it thousands of times. She rounded off the beaches and the cliffs, traced the circumference of the basalts and the salts, surrounded the sands and the rocks, and when the flame stopped trembling, it became steady as a lighthouse beacon because it was no longer sustained by the wax that softened with the heat of the sun and Estenia's hand, but instead it was her very fist that was being consumed. She understood her life's meaning. She recognized that Princess Anne had never given her a ring, but yet the preparations had been meaningful as part of a well-lived life.

The flame consumed her hand and later her arm and forearm and her entire body. Her dress burnt, her flesh and her entire skeleton were consumed, but the flame kept shining always, without ever burning out. The bony one stopped following her; she had Estenia, but not her candle, and it was the only time since she had arrived in the islands that she did not achieve what she wanted.

Estenia circled the island again and again. She recited the story of Prometheus who had stolen fire from Vulcan so as to give it to mankind, and when the inhabitants of the island saw her pass, they asked, astonished, "Where does that firefly that passes by on the beach every night get so much light?"

Tarsilia

Twice a year, Iridia wrote her mother three identical letters that she sent by different methods. One, on the slow boat that returned after leaving provisions in the islands. A second, in the pocket of one of the sailors who arrived on the tourist yachts. And the third, she deposited in the mailbox that James Colnett had left behind centuries ago and that was used by the English whalers and was still a desolate yet effective post office that fulfilled its mission of connecting with the world's most distant ports.

Perhaps one of them, Iridia thought, would reach her mother's hands. Many times, all three arrived together, and Tarsilia read them as if they were three different letters, because they were written in the morning, in the afternoon, and at night and they retained the color of the hours. They were simple letters, full of Iridia's spirit. They seemed like the continuation of a conversation interrupted by a drawn out sigh, or by a discreet cough that was the hawking that loosened and spat out the knot that formed in a throat squeezed by absence. The letters had the air of the islands and one could see in them the flight of the boobies, the redbill tropicbirds, the frigate birds and the gulls, the slither of the iguanas on the rocks, the philosophizing of the tortoises under their shells, the disintegration of the waves on the sand, and one could see the people dragging their customs and their occupations, with their happiness and their sorrows, in such a way that Tarsilia already knew all of the islands' inhabitants. She identified with many of them and she never lost the secret hope that she might join Iridia for good.

It was a long time since Tarsilia had received a letter. Her maternal anxiety anticipated the arrival of the ships; before they could anchor she was rummaging around in vain in the dark holds. Iridia had written no letters for a long time; nevertheless, she seemed to be more present than ever in the air, purifying the unhealthy miasmas of the tidal estuaries, helping Tarsilia with the housework, mending the clothes, hauling water, playing hopscotch with her brothers and sisters on the rotten boards crossing the marsh.

One day, Tarsilia felt more vehemently the call of the islands that was like the strident tone of a ship's siren. Before its ululating call that drilled through the clouds and frightened the birds had died away, without consulting anyone (because it was maternal instinct, pure and simple that drove her) she put her husband's tailor shop up for sale, with all its rulers, scissors, needles, and dummies. She collected her meager washerwoman's wages and booked passage on a beat-up boat that was heading for the islands. She packed up with disproportionate haste everything in her house and said, like one announcing an outing to the beach, that the next day they were going to join Iridia.

Her husband grumbled and protested, but given that years ago they had tacitly exchanged clothing, so that he wore the starched petticoats and she the trousers well secured on her round hips, he did not try to oppose her. The children jumped for joy. The islands were a dream come true, they bore the color of the goodness that the family's dark days lacked. They missed Iridia and wanted nothing else than to go to the place where she was.

The neighbors in the slum organized a farewell dance and at dawn, the boat departed. Pitching with the drunkenness of the night before and making S's on the waves, it headed out to open sea. The crossing was slow and grinding, the sky poured into the sea and the sea sank in the sky, they became one and fused together, cut by the imperceptible line of the horizon. The boat, without much stability, would climb to the summit of a rollercoaster. When it descended, the travelers, having emptied their buffeted and shaken stomachs, lay on the deck, limp and fainting. The noise of the motors drowned out conversation. Tarsilia's children, oblivious to seasickness and other discomforts, took control of their freedom and set to inspecting the engine room and the holds, they swung from the railings to port and to starboard, they ran around the deck tripping over everything, they got into the pots in the kitchen and they stood in front of the captain, whom they regarded with innocent nerve and semi-curious respect. They seemed like Richard Hughes' children after they left the *Clorinda* to live with the pirates and make their lives miserable. The captain let them do as they pleased, thinking that the adults' seasickness was caused by their having lost the lawlessness of the child so as to live entangled in laws and principles, asking themselves the hows and the whens, keeping their hearts in a cage and complicating an ephemeral existence. The children looked at the ship's captain and saw that the only captain-like things about him were a baseball cap and an unlit pipe that he never smoked but only gnawed at, spitting out the splinters every few seconds. They played a few pranks and the captain enjoyed them, although he seemed strict and pitiless; they played cat and mouse the whole trip and, when the holds were almost empty because their hi-jinks had awakened voracious appetites, they were finally able to make out the sinuous line of the island that marked the end of the crossing.

Tarsilia and her family unloaded their copious and battered luggage and they stood a long time, openmouthed, contemplating the inhospitable and savage beauty of the beach, the transparency of the water, and filling their lungs with fresh air. When they emerged on tiptoe from their astonishment at so much gratuitous beauty, they got down to work.

On a few of the islands there were still the remains of the large installations built by the Norwegians in the twenties, when they began to establish colonies and tried to settle permanently, clearing the higher elevations of the islands in order to plant. They were going to live off of fishing and the export of codfish. In the first months, they worked tirelessly, plucking from the land and the sea the finest fruits. But they fished so unrestrainedly that the cod noticed the ruthless hunt. Using implausible tacking maneuvers, the fish escaped from the nets, and thus the use of the foul-smelling and milky Scott's Emulsion—the stigma borne by a whole generation of skinny children—began to decline.

With the passage of time, the Norwegians forgot about fishing, about the seeds they had planted and the costly installations that at one time they had built with such fervor. Enthusiasm slowly became tedium and melancholy slackened the robust muscles that they had earlier displayed. They succumbed to the curse of the islands. They were unable to adapt or else the islands didn't want them. Their sturdy constitutions slackened with alcohol and nostalgia. The good intentions of fleeing the old world and its stunted precepts spilled out on the sand. They began to desert the burning beaches, and those who said they were only taking a short, necessary vacation never came back. The few who stayed spent the hours and the days sitting on the seashore, waiting for the ship that would come to rescue them. No matter if it was the Phantom Ship that would carry them to the country of death.

Tarsilia was a woman full of energy and of children, eternally young and perennially strong; she was capable of felling the island carob trees to build a house. Her bones endured tiredness and her muscles fatigue as the Norwegians of yesteryear had done. Her life was dedicated to the wellbeing of her family, so that as soon as the long voyage was over, she was one of the first to disembark, stiff from the inactivity on board and bored with so much moving water. Surprised that Iridia was not waiting for her on the dock, she began to move all the bundles that contained her home.

Between comings and goings, she asked everyone about Iridia's whereabouts and everyone dodged the issue or evaded the question until San Pío Pascual, as the most appropriate one and at Brigita's suggestion, spoke to her of resignation and other nonsense that Tarsilia couldn't bring herself to understand. Santa Livina, upon learning that Tarsilia was Iridia's mother, looked at her with disdain and confused her with the worst possible misgivings, until at last some sympathetic person took pity on her and told her that according to Miss Estenia, who was the last person to have seen her, Iridia had disappeared walking on air.

Tarsilia, dissolved in tears, sat down on one of the boxes in which her cups and plates had arrived and bitterly lamented the disappearance of the best of her children. Everyone cried for her. Tarsilia remained seated without occupying her hands with anything other than gathering the tears that gushed as copiously as Brigita's spring, and thus she remained during the longest time she could remember having been still, and when the last tear dried and she shook the sorrow out of her skirt as if it were crumbs of the most bitter bread she would ever eat, she saw the bony one who was spying on her from behind the rocks; she recognized her, and she set to work frenetically in order to win the race so that the egg—which perhaps she had already placed inside her—would burst, struggling so that it wouldn't enter her flesh, dying to take the lead in the decisive marathon to see who could do more, and more deeply.

She did not yet feel the poison in her body when she planted four trunks of carob wood in the sand. When they were solid enough to withstand the wind, she covered them from top to bottom with remnants of leftover boards from the old Norwegian buildings. She built a roof with pieces of zinc sheeting. To one side of the house she made a pen for the rooster and the five hens that had barely survived the rigors of the slow crossing; she gave them water and food, she stretched their legs and ruffled their feathers, while the inhabitants of the islands, sitting together at a prudent distance—so as not to offer help, which anyway was no longer necessary—saw how the building rose, how the woman did and undid, how she sawed and hammered, how she crouched down and stood up, while her husband, with every good intention of helping, had lagged behind and fallen asleep a good while ago, wrapped up in the tiredness of a forced voyage.

The bony one, on the other side of the people who were watching, didn't let Tarsilia out of her sight, alert for the first lapse she might have so she could come close and get the egg into her.

Meanwhile the rice was cooking on the improvised stove installed by the door of the house. Tarsilia went fishing, she threw the nets, going into the water up to her shoulders, and the fish came in heaps. They let themselves be caught, suffocating and lashing their tails, they let themselves be opened up to take out their intestines, and they let themselves be scaled, losing their shirts. Tarsilia ran back, ground the small, hot red peppers, chopped a pile of onions so as to have an excuse for her tears, sliced tomatoes, fried fish, and set plantains to roast on the coals. The oglers attracted by the scent of the food and by the improvised little sign that the children had written with a bit of charcoal on a board: *mariner's grill, S/. 10 per plate*, ate and ate again, taking turns at the wobble-legged table, licking their fingers and catching even the last grain of rice that the finches wanted to steal. Everyone ate, even Richardson, who lived on canned foods for want of hotdogs and hamburgers.

Tarsilia was running a crazy race with the one dressed in black who tried to get close to her by any means. Sometimes Tarsilia felt as if she were stepping on her heels and pulling on the colored ribbons that tied off her braids, but she managed to shake herself, using all her strength to dump her on any old corner in her path. As evening fell, she kept working, although with less spirit. Her muscles and her bones began to resent their mistreatment. She sat down for a moment to eat something, and that was her downfall, because while one of her children brought a plate of the mariner's grill from the wobble-legged table to the overturned box where she was sitting, the rotten one who was lying in wait won the race and got into her food. She knew it when she speared the oh-so-white meat of the cod to carry it to her mouth: there was the black one lodged among the vertebrae beside the tiny bones of the pale spine. She knew it when she cut the slice of tomato: there was the dun-colored one sitting on the pink-colored pulp. She knew it when she began to eat the rice: there was the dark one within the whiteness of every little white grain. She knew it when she cut the plantain: there was the gray one, lying down in the center as if it were a coffin. All the food had the taste of her sorrow at the death of her daughter and of knowing that she was going to depart following that child, leaving the others abandoned. She had to go, without having finished her work; there was no alternative.

Tarsilia finished her food, making an effort so as not to cough up the bolus of anguish, and tried to go on with her work. But when she went to the site where she had begun to build her house, she found that there, too, the leaden one was already in residence. She crouched between the joints of the boards and under the pieces of zinc, and when Tarsilia went to the improvised chicken coop, she saw that the opaque one had already placed herself on the rooster's spurs and gotten in between the hens' feathers. Afterward, Tarsilia felt her making herself comfortable inside her own organism. She felt the pains of childbirth that came not from her womb but from the soul's nerve, from the ganglia of consciousness, from the neurons of the spirit, from the buried pain of the child, because children hurt and they are the true owners of every Tarsilia's death. She felt the loss of Iridia in her bones, she felt her absence with more intensity than she had when she let her emerge from her bloody insides.

She had not been the same since she had sat down to eat her mariner's grill: sorrow had gotten into her body. She had always felt the need to discharge her energy so that her life force would come out transformed into sweat. Now she needed to keep working to expel the ill humors that began to rot her insides, humors that were simply tears detoured from the well-worn path from womb to eyes that sought a way out through the pores of her dark skin.

She was not yet well settled enough to devote herself to

gossip although she was dying to learn what the neighbors with whom Iridia might have lived were really like. She wanted to know more details about her daughter's life, to know how she walked on air, what dress she was wearing, what she had in her hands, if she seemed sad or contented, and to know if she went of her own will or if other unknown forces took her.

At the last minute, the neighbors offered to help her, but then they immediately stopped working because they began to see the maneuvers of a ship approaching the islands, and when the ship anchored, they saw that it was the same one on which Iridia had arrived. It lowered boats and more boats, full of blue sailors who waved from afar. As soon as she saw them, Tarsilia went to take more fish out of the sea. The fish came in heaps, Tarsilia piled them up on the sand, she cut off their heads with a sure blow of the machete so as not to see their eyes where sorrow crouched, she opened them up and pulled out their entrails, but she was more careful than before, because she knew that the bile was swollen with a presentiment and for that reason she took it out with more care and she threw it far away as if to cause the sharks indigestion and, right there, squatted on her heels, she washed the fish. The tailor cut them into pieces and all of them together fried and seasoned the plates heaped with food that disappeared within moments. The children came and went from the improvised stove to the palates of the hungry sailors. And when these had satisfied their hunger and stretched out in the sun they looked like an immense blue whale dreaming its dreams of distant ports. Tarsilia and her family sat down to count the money earned, which was more than sufficient to cover the costs of the voyage and its great hardships, while the one dressed in mourning kept watch on her trembling quarry.

At night, when the children slept and their bodies floated in the region comprised of wakefulness, the absurd, premonitions, and the past, from the bar next door one could hear chunks of music that the wind undertook to scatter like colored paper and that came flying out of an old RCA Victor victrola with a crank handle that someone had brought to the islands. The notes arrived in single file, interrupted by the wind, at Tarsilia's bedside. She tossed and turned uneasily, wrestling with the sorrow that fought to take over the last bastions of sleep; unable to avoid it, in spite of all her efforts, her feet tapped the rhythm of the music that came over from the bar where the sailors from the afternoon were drinking.

"Lie still!" thundered her husband, aching with sleepiness and all the hustle and bustle.

"Still? When I'm dead!" protested the woman wiped out by sorrow. After a brittle silence, she proposed that they go out for a beer.

"You're crazy! I'm dead tired, I could sleep for a whole year!" her husband responded, turning his back. He wrapped himself up in the sheets and carrying them on his shoulders, he entered the corridor of dreams and shut the door. Tarsilia was left alone and abandoned to the mercy of the pallid one who managed to seep through the gaps in the old boards, and before her terrified eyes, she put on the husband's pajamas as if wanting to possess her, but Tarsilia jumped, got out of bed, grabbed up some clothing and dressed in a hurry, running as if pursued over to the music's murky dive.

The place was full of drunken, nostalgic sailors. When they saw her arrive, they all crowded around. Tarsilia repressively smacked away the lustful hands that tried to envelop her as if they were the seaweed of a shipwreck, as if she were already at the bottom of the ocean, as if in reality she were already dead. The old RCA Victor sang a song that seemed written for her. The bony one opened a path between the men and when she was close to Tarsilia she pushed her into the arms of the brutal night and its consequences.

When the time came to leave the islands and the air was murky, the sailors, haggard and sad, picked themselves up heavily off the bar and Tarsilia understood that there was no longer any hope. She would never escape from her sorrow, the bony one had already claimed her as her own; it was all the same to her, she could cease to be who she was anywhere in the wide world.

The next day, in bed, the tailor began to unpick the stitches of one eye and then the other. He saw that the light of day did not come through the usual gaps, mending as always the walls with patches of dawn sunshine. Surprised, he took longer than he should to remember that he no longer lived in the old house in the slum, but in the islands, in a half built house where his wife had taken him, wrenching him off, as if he were a button, from the place where he had always been sewn. He saw himself counting the money they'd earned and smiled contentedly. He could begin a new life full of promise. He waited a long time, surprised not to hear the customary racket of pots and pans, of open doors and brooms with which his wife bustled around every morning as soon as it got light. He reached out a hand looking for her warm body and found only the cold sheets. He thought that Tarsilia had perhaps gone shopping, but on this island there were no shops where money might disappear. He saw the pile of bills still on top of the cookie box. He thought that maybe his wife had gone to get fish from the sea; he turned over his pillow and continued sleeping.

He woke up again after a few hours. The unusual silence inside his house bothered him and it surprised him that no one said anything about any kind of breakfast. He heard the muffled voices of his children, happy that no one was making them get up, and only when he began to hear an animated noise of voices in the street did he realize that the day was far advanced and that it was shameful to be still between the sheets. He remembered like a nightmare the shreds of music of the night before, and Tarsilia's intemperate insistence on going out. He became angry and shouted for her. He got up, worried. The stove's ashes were cold. To confirm it, he put his hand into them and was left staring, astonished, at the charcoal soot between his fingers that was like a portent of mourning and sorrow.

The rest of the luggage still to be unloaded remained intact, just as Tarsilia had left it the night before. Without washing, still fasting, his skin without water and his belly without food, the tailor and his children set about looking for her.

They went out onto the street asking everyone the whereabouts of the woman who had made the mariner's grill a few hours after landing, of the woman who was wearing a dress with yellow flowers and who had two long braids tied with colored ribbons, of the woman who was attractive without being pretty and had the same air and the same eyes as Iridia. Upon learning that she was Iridia's mother, the people began to search high and low. They went to the beaches, they climbed the high cliffs, they returned to the pier. They searched for her among the worm-eaten trunks, they climbed up to the highlands, they pushed aside the vegetation and looked among the wild orchids, the ferns and the old *licopodios*. They searched among the palo santo trees and the mosses that floated in the wind like ghosts' wings. They spread out across the whole island, calling for her with huge, strident yells. All of the sorrowing people shouted for her, piercing the air until they left it like a sieve. The echo carried urgent telegrams but returned only Tarsilia's name.

All was in vain. At nightfall, her husband and children gave up in defeat and sat down at the door of the half-built house looking at each other and feeling sorry for their respective abandonment. The search continued a few days longer, but still in vain. The luggage remained in a corner without ever being opened.

From time to time, the devastated family would sit on the island's highest cliff hoping in silence that some wave might bring, enveloped in its foam, the remains of a dark skinned body or perhaps the remnants of a dress with yellow flowers, but all was in vain. They never heard of her again.

It never occurred to them to look there, or on the morning of that first day, they might have seen far off, far, far off, like a strange vision, on the line without end of the horizon, the ship of the thousand sailors moving away, writing with hurried strokes on the blue chalkboard of the sky the words of farewell that Tarsilia sent back, fleeing her sorrow, touched by death, orphaned by the orphanhood of her daughter. The words rose with the gray smoke of the chimney and the wind undertook to destroy them so as to cleanse the sky of human sadness.

Tarsilia both left and did not leave on the ship, because as soon as she was on board, the egg of sorrow burst its bitter shell and spread its cancer. Her flesh disappeared as Alirio's had disappeared into the sand, as Estenia had been consumed by the flame, and when nothing remained but a piece of her perforated heart, the sailors, tired of seeing a yellow flowered dress that blew around like a leaf in a storm and wasn't good for anything, got sick of looking at it and kicked it into the water.

Brigita

When Brigita came and settled in the islands, everything was in blessed peace and accord between her and her neighbors, between her and her work, between her and the pure, pure air of the islands. She would get up at dawn and stoop over the earth to fell with her scant menopausal strength the *lechosos* and the *uñas de gato*, fighting the scrub for a place to sow the plants nourished by the faint drizzle of the early mornings. She also took care of a few hens and a pair of goats. She used her time and skill to treat *espanto*, those soul-freezing frights, on Fridays and Tuesdays. With a few papaya seeds, she removed the amebas from the intestines of a long line of patients, but she only removed the most bothersome and rebellious ones; the others she left in the body so that it could learn to tolerate them and, once they were domesticated, they might be integrated into the organism the way fatness or tiredness are integrated. She soldered more than a few bones with a thick ointment that she prepared with the fat of a tapir and she treated the sterile women of the islands who multiplied more and more every day ever since the appearance of a strange curse that Brigita could not combat. She had dedicated herself to these needs out of a vocation as deep as the vocation of Estenia, or Fritz, or Alirio. She had been initiated into this art through a traditional inheritance and because the medical doctors' treatments always seemed to her the real witchcraft. She could not understand how it was possible that, when one swallowed a little pill, the pill would know the exact spot to which it should head so as to ease a pain or cure a diseased organ. Brigita asked herself how it was possible that a pill could travel toward the head, stop in the throat without slipping way down inside, or go without the least hesitation to the kidneys or the bladder; the one thing she could understand was the working of pills for constipation or diarrhea. She asked herself, "How can anything this itty-bitty have the intelligence or the understanding not to take the wrong path?" That was the real witchcraft, not the waters that entered the body and bathed its interior, curing ailments, so to speak, as they went.

After the freshwater spring appeared, who knows how or when, everything changed for her. She felt herself privileged, humbly singled out by God or by luck. She exchanged grateful looks with the one-eyed spring. From time to time, she cleaned off the white cream that appeared on the surface of the hole, which was not cream, but the residue of the impassioned papers written by Alirio before he disappeared.

The water flowed fresh and courteous, softening the volcanic soil and slaking the thirst of the settlers as if it knew the reason and the mission behind its strange origin.

Brigita knew better than anyone the secrets of the plants and their mysterious affinities with the wind, the sun, the moon, and the position of the stars in the firmament. She could pull up by the root the ills and ailments of the body with the same ease she pulled weeds from her garden. People said that her hand was an extension of the hand of God. She spent long hours making unguents, ointments, and potions for the few sicknesses that appeared from time to time in the islands, given that it was the winds' task to expel any illness toward the mainland infested with microbes and bacteria. Mothers asked her frequently for amulets against the evil eye for the few children who remained, and she protected them by making cord necklaces from which she hung a cockscomb. Stomachache, measles, whooping cough, and other ailments that from time to time snuck through the dead calms of the sea, disappeared immediately with her miraculous tisanes. She knew how to make the water of the seven spirits that did everyone good, and she had packets with every kind of herb and root regularly sent from the mainland on the same run that brought Santa Livina's magazines, letters for Estenia or for Alirio, and some large envelopes with foreign stamps for the man who spent his life with the giant cacti.

As soon as she received her orders of herbs, Brigita would hurry to soak them in the waters of her spring so that they would be fresh and lush as if newly picked from the plants. Brigita was unable to do wrong, she could only do good. The bony one knew she was marked for a certain year, day, and hour and she left her in peace because Brigita's end would not be the work of her bony hands but of fanaticism and intolerance.

Brigita was a healer, bone-setter, skilled at reducing dislocated joints, and gleaner according to the circumstances. She always got the diagnosis and the treatment right, partly by intuition and partly from knowledge. There was always some patient in her house asking for help, so much so that the hospital, recently inaugurated in a memorable ceremony (which included an opening speech and another speech at closing, along with a ribbon-cutting, photographs, band, and fireworks) remained intact and virgin, free from contamination or cries of pain, modern and well-equipped, with medications lined up on the shelves in closed, sealed boxes, with the

174

equipment still in plastic bags, with the syringes and the rubber gloves still in their packaging, waiting in vain for someone to need them. The one thing that was old and worn out through continuous use was a deck of cards with naked women on the backs (not because they were hot, but because that was its owner's preference) used to kill time and pass the long hours by the doctor and the nurses who lived with their hands folded, yawning and drinking soda pop, waiting for the patients who, after the inauguration, never appeared.

The payments of the grateful sufferers who were cured as if by magic, the sale of her few fruits and vegetables, and the orders for beverages, ointments, and syrups made Brigita a rich woman—but how could a woman of the islands, where wealth was in proportion to the lean soils that were given away to anybody, to the rudimentary methods of cultivation, to the primitive pharmacy that had no aspirations, to the system of exchange and the dribbling spring, be rich? The money, notable for the absence of large bills, piled up in the bottom of an empty saltine can that was always open. Brigita's wealth was in her prestige and with that prestige came power, and with power, envy.

As soon as the spring appeared, the neighbors hurried to make canals so that the scarce liquid would also irrigate their lands. But the water was resistant to following another course: it hopped over the stones, climbed the hummocks, flowed backwards and spilled lazily over Brigita's land, but no one else's. The neighbors tried to channel it through improvised bamboo pipes but the water churned restlessly and then it went back. They brought tinplate gutters from the mainland but the water, which knew that its value was higher than that of milk or of *aguardiente*, did not allow itself to be channeled: it was born free and so it would continue, forever. Besides, Brigita's much envied and talked-about spring was no fountain or even close, it was scarcely a tenuous weeping of the basalt rocks. It welled up drop by drop and collected in a hollow that could be covered with the hands. It spilled over, following its route, its own route traced beforehand; it moved as if it were a worm crawling over the earth wherever its own instinct might guide it.

The water of the spring had a special flavor because it passed through the mint plants that grew along its length and all around the spring itself, like the lashes of the spring's eye that looked at the peoples' thirst and refreshed the throats of those who sang. It was the sweetest, most crystalline of all the waters of the islands, perhaps because when the water appeared out of Alirio's tenderness and impotence, it made it so that springtime, with all its verdure and its fruits, also became a settler on the island; the trees grew with a city of birds and the tiny seeds that slept in the soil woke up in a poem of cabbages and lettuces and turnips and parsley, as if this were not the dry soil of the islands.

After that, Brigita's small plot was no longer called a plot, and although it retained the same dimensions and the same boundaries, it began to be called a farm. But so that everything wouldn't be a paradise—because the bony one was in the middle of it all—the farm bordered the dry, thorny plot of San Pío Pascual and Santa Livina who didn't bother to clear or plant, saying they were both unable and unwilling, because both of them concentrated their efforts and their sleepless nights on other sacred, specific missions which were not those of cultivating the earth like vulgar laborers. They were in the islands with a spiritual and eternal mission, namely that of saving souls from sin.

When Brigita's neighbors walked through their uncultivated plot, they imagined that it was the true vale of tears and that with their mere presence they were saving souls and more souls that they could string like pearls to make an ethereal necklace that would serve as a receiving line when they took the final step from this world to the next through the narrow celestial pass of the heavens. But, in spite of everything, and putting aside their mystical longings, when they saw the fertility of Brigita's plot, they wondered every night why the spring refused to divide and subdivide itself to moisten even a few inches of their thirsty land. They well knew that the direct cause was not Brigita. She had never opposed the improvised aqueducts of bamboo and tinplate; on the contrary, she had wanted to collaborate with everyone. And thinking every night and all day long, they reached the bitter conclusion that their relations with the Lord above were not what they hoped.

God was blessing Brigita with his powerful right hand and blessing them any which way with his left. And as is natural and human, they grew resentful of the Creator who made things so unintelligible, to say the least, and they set out upon the intricate path of predestinations and other fine threads and metaphysical complications that corrode the haughty spirit. Full of sacred professional zeal, they began to look at Brigita in their own way, without managing to understand how the one who was called the Just of the Just could bless so generously she who merely took care of the bodies—putrid and insubstantial matter—and yet barely noticed those who took care of the immaterial souls that were the sacred receptacles of the spirit. Wounded, Santa Livina asked herself, "Why do these things have to happen when from any perspective and by reason of any intelligence her work is infinitely inferior and proletarian compared to ours, given that, as they say—parodying the Gospel—Brigita is not even worthy to unbuckle our sandals?"

"What sandals?" San Pío Pascual asked, irritated at so much whining.

"It is understood that they are not sandals, but boots, but a word to the wise is sufficient," answered Santa Livina, going over and over the matter of why to her and not to them, since in the end, a healer with her herbs and concoctions was still practically a witch, while a priest with his aunt, no matter who it might upset, were holy because of their acts and also their respective baptismal names, which marked them from the beginning of their lives with the indelible seal of what they would be later on.

Holiness was a family matter. Every member of the family put the San or the Santo at the beginning, in such a way that eventually, the younger generations opted to carry their holiness as a surname.

When San Pío Pascual came into the world, Providence deigned to open two doors: designs are designs, Santa Livina affirmed; from the one emerged naked and frightened little San Pío Pascual toward the cradle, and through the other departed, trembling and bundled up, his mother toward her tomb. She was dragged by the pallid one. The son came out hollering and the mother left crying, not wanting to follow the footsteps of death.

"One soul leaves and another arrives," was the sole comment of the sister of the deceased, who was Santa Livina, hastening to pick up the orphan.

And lest idle tongues in the neighborhood be many and very long, so that there would be a record for posterity and for the neighbors in the town where they lived, the same day they buried her sister, when the relatives had not yet left the house of mourning and the body was stretched out on the living room table, Santa Livina turned up— tearful, circumspect, and entirely wrapped in black—at the office of the family doctor, and she asked him to issue a medical certificate stating that her virginity was intact and untouched. The doctor indicated that she should undress and lie down on the examining table.

"Undressed and lying down?" shouted Santa Livina, offended and humiliated, with a shriek that could be heard up to the heavens. She felt herself at the pinnacle of the most desperate situation she could endure.

The doctor, with miraculous patience, because for this he had his years and his experience, explained to her, paternally and professionally, that it was a matter of a purely routine exam.

"This isn't pure routine, it's pure soliciting!" Santa Livina yelled, her cheeks burning, protecting those parts that were in danger as if she were facing a satyr. She refused to listen to any explanation. She went out, giving the door a terrible slam, and she ran as if she were being pursued toward the confessional of the nearest church, and there she stayed for hours and hours, making a nuisance of herself until she finally obtained what she was after, which was a certificate with the seals of the parish house and the signature of the long-suffering priest in which it was recorded that, to whom it might concern, the herein named Miss Lady Santa María Livina and the other surnames, after having passed with flying colors a catechetical examination, swore by the salvation of her soul and by the eternal rest of her sister Santa Leonila that, without having been touched or (worse) examined by a man's hand, the signatory below testified and certified her entire virginal condition and also that the child that she was going to raise from this date forward, was her blood nephew, legitimate son of her sister, and not the misbegotten fruit of any step wrongly placed and wrongly permitted.

When they brought the child to the one who from then

on would be his adopted mother, in her barren insides there awoke a ferocious maternal instinct and when she began to take care of him, the whole house, from the entry hall to the roof, was thrown into confusion by her hysterical yells, because upon taking off his diapers, which were soaked, she saw something horrible and hollered, appalled: "Oh my God! This baby is sick! Call the doctor! It has a tumor growing between its legs!"

All of the neighbors came solicitously to her aid, setting her straight with the greatest small-town patience. Astonished, Santa Livina heard how it was that babies were made. She asked if the dogs in the street did that in plain sight of everybody. They told her yes. She asked if her sister Santa Leonila had done that in the street. They told her no, that people did that in bed and they explained in passing the specific differences between boys and girls and between men and women. Santa Livina opened her eyes enormously wide, she started crying all over again for her dead sister, and from then on she was left with an unsatisfied curiosity. Hours later, the house shook with another round of screaming and yelling: "Oh my God! Call the doctor! I'm lost!"

Until the doctor arrived, Santa Livina was a pure lamentation for having accepted the role of mother which was different from what the poems said. It was a difficult and painful calling. She lamented having forgotten the most important thing but she didn't say what that was... The doctor arrived and found her desperate. Santa Livina had begun to love San Pío Pascual not as a nephew but as her own child. Between labored hiccups, blushing, she asked the doctor to, without a moment's delay and if possible without anesthesia, immediately make the corresponding holes in her breasts so that the milk which was waiting, and with which she needed to nurse San Pío Pascual, who was bawling with hunger, could come out.

"Hurry! Here are the needles."

Stunned, the doctor wracked his brains trying to remember if at any time in his long professional career he had encountered a similar case. Once again, the well-meaning neighbor women explained the process of lactation, and baby bottles, and, while they were at it, they taught her about diarrhea with teething, and colds, measles, and other sicknesses. When Santa Livina had lost all that remained of her innocence and put her feet firmly on the ground, she devoted herself to taking care of the child as best she could.

Her certificate of virginity hung above the cradle, next to the picture of the Guardian Angel. With the passage of time, she molded the soul and the inclinations of the child, so that when he grew up, he set out determinedly and without any hesitation upon the only path he had before him: the seminary.

Upon arriving in the islands, that same certificate, yellowing and made almost illegible by the rigors of the climate and the passage of time, was at the head of San Pío Pascual's hammock, but it mattered little. Nobody was interested in knowing his parentage. They were almost a single person: Santa Livina was the idea and San Pío Pascual was the action.

From the time she appeared, Brigita's death was already bound up in the lives of the nephew and the aunt. The rumor that she might be a witch began taking shape when the mysterious spring appeared and refused to irrigate the plot belonging to the two pious goody-goodies. Masked and covered, the intrigue emerged from their house, but they kept quiet a long time, because they knew what Brigita meant to the islands' inhabitants.

One day, the *Floreana* which had always appeared every so often bringing necessary and eagerly awaited provisions, didn't arrive at the port, and hunger, which is the worst advisor, stirred the wagging tongues and spurred San Pío Pascual and Santa Livina on more forcefully than at other times, making them say whatever they pleased and making their overworked livers secrete old resentments. And when they set out for the church that had not yet been built, during the Sunday religious service that the women attended so they could be seen well dressed and groomed, taking along the men who also liked to see the show, San Pío Pascual, casually and at the same time oracular, like a good Christian, said of Brigita, who was not present because she was always busy, "It could well be that she cures the sick with the aid of a someone who is not precisely an angel nor an archangel…"

And then, without meaning to say exactly what he said, because they were in the house of God where all, he said, were children of the same father and coheirs to the same glory, but rather because he could no longer find anything more to say, because he couldn't even sermonize and his flabby intestines were pealing for the dead as if the bony one were hanging from the clapper and he couldn't send the parishioners home with such a short sermon, still fasting in body and spirit, he told them in passing, so to speak, just like that, like any other anecdote, that, "...although it had to do with the distant past, yet it would serve as well in the present, because humanity has always been the same as it is now and ever since, and long ago, and to be more exact and precise—because one can't speak any old way in this house of God, which has yet to be built because the parishioners busy themselves with everything save making a worthy edifice—in the Middle Ages, and who could be sure that it wasn't also done in other ages, and perhaps also in these same days, well, to safeguard religion, which is and continues to be the principal duty of all Christians, they built giant pyres in the public squares, and this happened everywhere, so as to burn witches alive, because it was necessary to purify people's beliefs of strange practices and demonic enchantments that have always been condemned and that continue to be prohibited by the Church, because the practices of these diabolical women, which exist in every corner of the planet, attack the principles of the Holy Mother Church, and given that in times past and who knows if also in the present day, it is known and understood by all that they flew in the night on broomsticks, and that, as I already said, long ago they went out at twelve midnight on the dot to meet at their infamous witches' sabbaths where they committed every kind of impure and iniquitous act that the tongue and decent customs refuse to mention, and they also sacrificed young children, and everyone knows and understands that for many years there have been no young children in these islands, and that the reason could be a punishment from God for sins committed or for refusing to build the church, and if it isn't a punishment it is something else which may be called witchcraft, and going back to the witches of times past, history tells us that they drank the hot blood of young children, and who can be sure that these vile acts have disappeared the world over; and probably, it could be that in these same places where we live, forgotten by human progress, there may be among us one of them, a witch masked and sly like the witches of the Middle Ages, but since now times have changed, they no longer fly on broomsticks but instead do other things like medicines and potions that are the work of the devil and his followers, because it is impossible to read the thoughts and know what happens in the conscience of one who does not practice the holy sacraments, and without wanting to accuse anyone, because that is not the mission of he who speaks to you, but rather to watch over the good of all, because it is not necessary to say the name of one who is never present in this place, but instead up there on the hill..."

At this point, the whole audience, which was half asleep, woke up completely and began to look around to see who it was that was missing, and then, only then, putting two and two together, did they manage to understand what San Pío Pascual's sermon was about, for never since he had been in the islands had he delivered such a long, round-about sermon. He was saying that Brigita was a witch and their hair stood on end and their minds, too. They left the service uneasy, with a bitter taste between their teeth. They went away to think and ponder, each after his own fashion: *And if Brigita were really a witch…?*

The ship, which was the same one on which Alirio arrived one day looking for his muse; the same in which Estenia arrived to make the myth of Prometheus a reality; the same in which Iridia put in to port in search of an impossible love; the same in which Tarsilia came with her children and with her house on her back; the same in which Fritz made his cruises in search of new species of *Opuntia echios* and in which San Pío Pascual and Santa Livina arrived hunting for emaciated souls, did not arrive at any port. The *Floreana* never arrived, only the news that it was wrecked close to the coast with its entire cargo of provisions. The anguish of the dry season and its hunger were the last straw. The words that San Pío Pascual said in the Mass remained floating in the salty air, forming a cloud swollen with storm. One person, only one out of everyone on the island, came out the beneficiary of these catastrophes, and it was none other than Brigita, who could sell the produce of her garden at whatever price she pleased…

The words of San Pío Pascual, which emerged from

the black thoughts of Santa Livina, followed the same movements as the waves that crashed against the rocks of the cliffs. Then the bony one began her task, whispering in people's ears and preparing the path along which she would carry Brigita; and with that was born distrust, and with distrust, suspicion, and with suspicion was born fear, and with fear was born madness.

Might it not be Brigita with her healer's arts—she who had stopped being a healer to be transformed, violently, into a witch—who had used the demonic and supernatural powers of one rejected by God, of a reprobate, of a diabolical one and an obsessive, to put her hands into the waters of the sea, infuriating the waves and provoking the shipwreck? Or perhaps she had bewitched the swordfish so that they would bore through the old hull of the *Floreana*? And the cures she performed every day, couldn't that maybe be the work of the Evil One to mark and stigmatize the people who used her services, and get back his own, pitching them into hell when they left this life? Who could be sure that Brigita, all alone in her domain, far from the houses of the town, had not made a pact with the devil? No one remembered ever seeing her prowling around in the vicinity of the church that had not yet been built, nor of the parish house that existed only in the dreams of San Pío Pascual and Santa Livina. And although they had had long conversations with Brigita about the spring and the way in which they wanted to channel it, from the moment in which the things that were said in the church—which had yet to be built—were said, it was as if the two parts in discord had never exchanged words, as if they had barely met during years of being neighbors, as if they had not seen her daily walking in the street. And old images and concepts and ideas were erased and different ones arose.

Brigita walked on the other side of the island, which was steeper and more precipitous, lonelier and darker, more winding and remote, as if it were the place for wicked dealings with the Evil One. And she walked during the night, solitary and fearful as an unquiet soul. Did she walk? Didn't she perhaps appear and disappear among the *orchillas* and the palo santos, her feet not touching the ground bristling with volcanic ridges that cut the soles? She walked very fast, she almost flew... Yes, she flew above the cliffs, never along the normal road of the respectable folk.

And she also traveled mounted astride an old broom, and although they had always seen her dressed in white and in light colors like the women of the islands, they began to see her dressed in black. And although they chatted and laughed with her and they were grateful for the water and they paid her for the treatments, they began to see her aged and toothless, with a hooked nose and perverse little eyes, the same eyes as the black rat that chased Iridia. And they heard her laughing, shrill, strident guffaws like the caw of the crows, when she came close to the few children that remained in the islands, as if the curse were her doing.

Little by little, like the shadows of the night, like the mental corruption of the innocent, like the disloyalty of friends, like the betrayal of those who love each other, the image of Brigita changed. The pupil itself was distorted upon seeing her pass, and people began to forget about things as obvious as when they stood in line for her to get rid of their toothache, lance the swellings of their ulcerated feet to banish the burrowing chigoe fleas with their eggs, stretch their abdominal and stomach muscles so that the mis-directed food might follow the well-beaten path from the dining table to the sewers. They forgot how the women in labor ran out of the hospital that had just been inaugurated, out of the grasp of the doctor, because he wanted them to lie down on a cold, aseptic table, legs splayed and tense, pathetic and terrified—and to make it even worse, with an enormous lamp over their private parts, which seemed like a gigantic eye through which all of the eyes of all the inhabitants of the islands peered, watching and criticizing the whole process of the birth and speculating about what might have happened before the birth, during the birth, and after the birth. And they forgot about how, leaving the hospital utterly petrified, they ran as fast as they could to place themselves in the hands of Brigita, who helped them push the painful bundle out of their insides in the time-honored position of their mothers and grandmothers, squatting or kneeling, natural and still in the most transcendental act of their lives, to receive the best gift that they could be given and which, terrible misfortune, had disappeared, although Estenia, before becoming a firefly, had put them onto the gringo

Richardson as the one to blame for there no longer being any births.

Brigita went on with her work, unaware of what was said of her behind her back, indifferent to certain whispers that she surprised in passing, without noticing that she no longer had any patients, believing rather that between her potions and the healthy air of the islands, they had managed to ward off forever all of the ailments and illnesses; but she was a little sad, because she had come upon the pallid one spying on her wherever she went.

It was the dreaded dry season. The spring continued to put out its little tear, but it stopped raining. The cattle wandered around looking for a useless pasture and exhibiting their ribcages like walking x-rays. The stunted dwarf evergreen oaks were covered with a fine, brownish-gray dust that got in people's throats and the pharmacist despaired, remembering the methylene blue that Estenia dumped onto her sheets. The *muyuyos* had disappeared, the ground was cracked like the hands of the old peasant women. The birds fanned themselves with their wings above the solid air that broke the rhythm of their flights. Only the spring continued flowing and it even seemed as if its thread had gotten thicker and its flavor were sweeter and more refreshing.

Fishermen and sailors came from all over with bottles and plastic jugs to carry away the water, and Brigita let them take it without charging anything. She had never heard of water being sold, she only made sure that there was neither waste nor abuse, not wanting to see repeated again the scene that the settlers of another island recounted, when the Baroness Wagner arrived and climbed into the only spring on the island, naked and with her bar of soap, sensual and lubricous and without caring that she was climbing into the drinking glass and the cooking pot of the few people who lived there back then.

Brigita's death was born with her, and the spring that appeared for her hastened her departure. It was impossible for those who believed themselves privileged yet were not to forgive her privilege. The same sadness as when Fritz died fell over the islands, and it was the sadness of knowing that the things with which one is born end up killing one, just as the sadness of his incomprehensible dryness killed Alirio.

The *Floreana* had followed the same vertical trajectory as the launch that carried Fritz and the five Danish scientists. It had gone down while its few sailors managed to get themselves to safety and tell the tale.

And it happened that the people also dried out like the land and they cracked with hatred, and when Brigita went down to the beach, without the hooked nose or the malevolent little eyes nor landing with the pole of the supposed broom, but instead with a basket of fruits and vegetables, then who knows who (maybe it was the bony one) whispered *the witch* and opened the closed door of the moment, scattering on the air grudges old and new. They remembered the sinister sermon of San Pío Pascual, who maybe said it without meaning to, but he said it. And when night arrived, pregnant with darkness and evil passions, the inhabitants of the island were prowling around Brigita's house with the bony one in the lead, walking on tiptoe and carrying a can of gasoline and a box of matches.

It didn't matter who they were, because it was everyone. They forced the door of the house which had no latch because it wasn't necessary and they dragged out the poor old woman who went to her death without understanding what was happening, scarcely trying to defend herself with her tongue which cracked like a whip, beating the shadows and the deaf ears. Brigita's eyes bulged with questions, all but popping out of her head. She kicked and scratched helplessly until they bound her and tied her hands with the shreds of her white dress. And they carried her that way to the center of the plaza, dragging her across the sand and the basalt rocks that still retained the stifling heat of afternoon. They tied her to an old carob trunk, the bony one passed them the gasoline, and they lit the fire.

Brigita struggled amidst the flames that wanted not to harm her but were unable to avoid it; timidly, they began to lick at her body and then they had to consume it, swallowing in the first mouthfuls her light colored clothes and her black hair; later they chewed, as if they were savoring the flesh and the charred bones. The remains of Brigita appeared and disappeared in the cloud of smoke, creating the most grotesque medieval scene in the center of the plaza. For a long time, a time prolonged interminably in shrieks, they heard entreaties, curses, and questions. A few women cried in anguish because Brigita took too long to die. Some of the men kept throwing dry branches onto the crackling blaze and they were consumed within seconds.

The bell of the church that was not yet built tolled a few weak peals calling the faithful to the evening Mass. No one went that day and so they did not see how San Pío Pascual spilled the wine, trying to control the nervous trembling of his hands that fell down on him in the moment of the offertory, while Santa Livina, the only person who attended the religious service, without ceasing to be also in the plaza hauling dry branches, prayed with her arms extended in a cross the blasphemous prayer of the Just Judge.

Little by little, Brigita turned black and scorched. The carob pole to which she was tied disintegrated into millions of sparks that flew like the ignis fatuus of a macabre evening. Brigita doubled over on herself. A cloud of smoke, white and stinking, grazed everyone's eyes, making them cry by force. The odor of roast meat penetrated all the empty kitchens and the image of Brigita eternally writhing amidst the blue and yellow flames was forever engraved on the retinas of the islands' inhabitants.

Then the bony one raked through the ashes and became furious because she could not find what she was looking for. After a while, a short shower fell, just enough to calm the bonfire and the furor of unleashed passions, and it was then that Brigita turned into smoke.

The smoke began to rise gently and when it was above

the highlands, over the plot that had been hers, it stretched out its gray arm and caught the spring. It rolled it up like a sheet of silver and the smoke stopped being smoke. Brigita became a cloud that rose slowly into the sky.

In the highlands, the carob trees scorched by the sun no longer held up the desiccated *orchillas* that barely moved in the wind when they saw the cloud pass and go away. In the lowlands, when only a mound of ashes was left, the men looked at their sooty hands and wanted to wash, but the seawater only left them dirtier. Then they went to the spring and when they reached out their hands looking for its moisture, they came up against entirely dry rocks, with the absolute dryness of Alirio when he struggled to write a poem. They scratched at the soil and they were terrified when they saw that the spring had disappeared as mysteriously as it had come.

In the clear sky, Brigita kept traveling. She was a cloud swollen with downpour. She seemed to be made of Bohemian crystal, she could dissolve in rain even with the gentle brush of a bird's wing. And she moved further away from the islands and she went singing a strange song through the Gobi, across the Sahara, to Kara-Kum and Nubia, she went to Colorado and the Atacama Desert and she never again returned to the islands until the day she learned that San Pío Pascual and Santa Livina had embarked for the mainland.

Richardson

The one person who, oblivious to the drama, didn't find out what was going on in the center of the plaza, was the owner of the Hot Cakes Bakery. Busy kneading and baking his big loaves, he didn't even notice the scent of roasted meat that got into every corner of the houses, spread to the other islands, and even reached the mainland like the macabre reminder of other centuries, a scent that remained in peoples' minds, unchanging and horrible. The blades of the enormous fans kept the singed smell from slipping into the aseptic, cold bakery, impersonal and tidy as a laboratory, from which it seemed impossible that bread with such home-baked warmth and flavor could emerge.

Richardson was the son and grandson of bakers. If he had lived in the time of heraldry, his coat of arms would have been a sack of flour or a mound of steaming cottage loaves or perhaps a bunch of wheat spikes, but it was the era of vitamins, plastic, and contraceptives. Richardson knew all the secrets of dough and all the states of leavening, of kneading and firing, but sadly, he didn't use them because the machines, and only the machines, enjoyed the pleasurable work of mixing and beating the dough, while he only kept watch and pushed the dry, cold buttons.

He came to the islands on a vacation tour organized especially for bakers, and was bewitched by the spell of the sea and above all by the suggestive legends that the guide told him about the large number of people who had mysteriously disappeared, one of whom was the Baroness Wagner, evaporated who knows how and under extremely compromising circumstances inside a web of international espionage. Richardson was touched by the story, and in trying to assemble the puzzle of the mystery of the disappearances, he expended hundreds of hours of rest and kilometers of conjecture. He didn't like the idea that the Baroness Wagner had been murdered by one of her lovers; he preferred to accept the hypothesis that she had fled in a Japanese submarine and must be living the licentious life of a devourer of men and of fortunes in some part of the world, hidden under a different surname, with the cover of cosmetic surgery and the help of geriatrics.

One year later, on the next tour, not for bread bakers this time but for donut makers, he returned to the islands and decided to camp at the bay of Los Perros. He got lost on purpose, because he needed to get lost if he wanted to dig up some sign related to the characters who lived in the islands during the turmoil of the Second World War. He walked all night until he reached the pirate caves without finding anything. They weren't places frequented by the baroness. He began to challenge the ground he had already covered, guiding himself by the sound of the yacht siren which demanded his presence. When the sun came out, and he was still looking for some kind of clue—because it was impossible to accept that he might find nothing— he saw among the high cacti a piece of cloth that danced, tossed around by the wind. He ran closer and could hardly believe his eyes, because he was immediately convinced that what he had before him was nothing less than a sign that the baroness had been there. He praised the perfect organization of the cruise which anticipated his desires, and it made no difference that the guide assured him that the baroness had frequented other islands. Many years had passed, the piece of fabric was in tatters, and it could well be that the wind had carried it or that the baroness had walked through these parts naked, *au natural*, leaving her clothing behind anywhere.

It seemed to be the remains of a blouse, because it

showed the irrefutable seams and shape of a sleeve. It had three very delicate buttons and of course it was impossible that it might belong to any of the women of the islands. On the upper part, the remains of what might once have been a filigree of lace were revealed at first glance. He knew from experience that this was not the kind of clothing worn by tourists. He was disconcerted at not knowing if what he had in front of him was a shirt or a blouse. He had to gather his conjectures and discard them one by one. The women who took cruises to the islands wore clothing planned in advance, sturdy and athletic as the tourist brochures suggested, and not this fabric that came apart at the touch of a finger.

He was convinced that the piece of fabric must have belonged to the baroness because just by touching it he felt a lustful jolt and he even saw her in said blouse, with the two upper buttons undone, so the opening of the neckline extended down to her belly. Barely keeping itself closed with the third button so that the wind might not take it off her body, worn with very short pants and a belt from which hung a real, miniature pistol. The blouse had to be hers. He took out his handkerchief, spread it over the sand, put the fabric on it and, folding them carefully, walked on as if he had found Morgan's treasure.

From that moment on he stopped enjoying the amenities of the cruise. He was not interested in the climate or the landscape, nor the fauna nor the flora, nor any of the other legends that were unrelated to the baroness. He counted the days and the hours until the return, so as to go back to his country as quickly as possible and find out for certain that what he had found was the baroness' blouse. He had fallen deeply in love with her, just as the tubercular lover who followed her around like a dog must have been, or any of the other men who were with her.

From his country, he would organize an expedition and he would find her, dead or alive. He would determine her whereabouts or touch her skeleton with his hands and he would build a tomb that would always have flowers, just as Doctor Ritter's tomb did whenever German tourists landed.

When the cruise was over and his traveling companions had said goodbye, wishing him luck in his projects, an eager and feverish Richardson arrived in the big city where he was interviewed by a reporter for a sensationalist magazine that agreed to help him in his enterprise, and which published an extensive report in which he appeared as the discoverer of a clue that would illuminate the mysterious disappearance of the exotic baroness which had occurred in the wild and distant islands.

The haggard bit of fabric was sent with the necessary precautions and considerations to a laboratory where a team of specialists in American antiquities fed the computer and—well sated with data—it digested the digestible and offered the following, sensational deposition which was published in the magazine and in other periodicals:

10.4.1. The material had been exposed for a long time in a saline environment. (Generally, islands are chunks of land surrounded by ocean water.)

10.4.2. The piece of fabric belonged to a blouse, not to a shirt, and thus was a feminine garment and in no way masculine. (The baroness was a woman.)

10.4.3. The original color of the garment was beige. (The baroness would have liked pastel shades.)

10.4.4. The material from which said garment had been made was natural silk of Indian origin. (Nothing so appropriate to a baroness as that she should have in her wardrobe a natural silk blouse.)

10.4.5. The size of said garment was equivalent to a size 10. (The baroness must have been tall and thin; had it been otherwise, had she been squat and chubby, she would not have had as many lovers as they say that she had.)

10.4.6. On said garment, a slightly dark stain could be seen on first glance. Once said stain was analyzed in a laboratory specially designed for that purpose, it was determined that the coloration corresponded to a mixture whose base was alcohol. (It was known that the baroness was not exactly abstemious.)

10.4.7. The buttons of the aforementioned garment were mother-of-pearl, of European manufacture. (The baroness came from Paris.)

These were, in sum, the most important conclusions reached

by the protracted and exhaustive examination, the full report of which was published in its entirety in the magazine along with photos of the islands and of Richardson, who became famous from one day to the next as if he had scored the decisive goal in a championship soccer game. And, still not satisfied—better put, egged on by the results of the report—he conceived the idea of sending said garment, along with the relevant biographical information about the vanished woman, to another laboratory that specialized in making the most famous restorations, in which the blouse was entirely remade, because once the wrapper was constructed, its contents could be found. Once the shell was reconstructed, the seed could be found. Once the skin was reconstructed, the marrow could be located.

While he awaited the results of the relevant data, he sank into an anguished anxiety and when the blouse was entirely restored and he had it in his hands, he decided to travel to a different city, and when he arrived, he settled himself close to one of the largest plastics factories in the world. There, elbow to elbow, a team of technicians set themselves the task of computing the anthropometric measurements of the former owner of the supposed blouse which had become the real blouse of the real baroness. Assisted by a collection of photocopies that he had been able to compile on his previous trips, taken from contemporary newspapers and from the photograph albums of those who lived with the baroness—although not on very good terms—he observed that in the photos she was not very well favored, she was no beauty, but she had a strange power of seduction, as all of her biographers wrote. She was not lovely, nor pretty, nor beautiful, but she could excite violent passions even from within yellowing papers and blurry photos. He was putting together the puzzle of the image that was traced on his retinas and he went back to waiting. He closed the bakery because journalists hounded him day and night, and it was impossible to concentrate on his thoughts and his erotic imaginings. He could do nothing other than think about her. He confused salt with flour, water with milk, the oven door with the window, the toilet with the armchair in the living room, the dough with the table, the buttons on the breadmaking machine with the buttons on his vest. He waited, obsessed, in expectation of what would emerge, while he chewed on his nails as if they were candied peanuts, staring at the telephone—which must ring *some* time—for hours at a time and waiting to hear the doorbell.

He lost a lot of weight in the long wait, putting on pallor and circles under his eyes as the fat of his skin trickled away along the tightrope of uncertainty. Smoking and taking long walks, he seemed like a father waiting for news of the birth of his first child. Then the appointed day came. The order arrived. It was a large cardboard box carried by four men, two on each side, walking solemnly as if they were carrying a coffin. And when Richardson signed the confirmation of delivery that would be paid for by the magazine along with the postage on the tourist brochures until the trail of the baroness produced results, he closed and locked the door and was alone. He began to open the box. His hands and all the rest of him trembled with emotion and curiosity as he took off the adhesive tape, lifted the protective seals and removed the Styrofoam bits. And when he finally managed to lift the lid of what really seemed like a casket made to measure for the most demanding dead man, he gave a shout of surprise and satisfaction: there was the fruit of his sleepless nights and his yearning; there lay the materialization of his dream, just as he had planned. There she was, stretched out, semi-naked, barely covered by the much-traveled silk blouse (partially open, just to the last button) smiling and defiant: the one and only Baroness, resuscitated and reconstructed to the smallest detail in a virtuoso show of technical skill. She was of a plastic material, like the true flesh and blood of the twentieth century. Dark-skinned, tanned by the tropical sun of equatorial lands, with a wig of short, black hair just like she had in the photographs in Margaret Wittmer's book and with the same exact features. She had experienced not a single change in the passage from photograph to sculpture, from the second dimension to the third dimension, from black and white to full color, at being transported from existential nothingness to a corporeal, ductile reality.

Richardson realized that he should behave very courteously and with refinement and that he must overcome with easy speech the obstacle of there not being a third person who could make the appropriate introductions. He was reluctant to look at her, still less to touch her; he almost felt himself before a *noli me tangere*. Some time passed during which he went around in circles, not knowing what to do, until he had to overcome his diffidence before the surprising encounter, and skipping over the rules of good manners—because curiosity was stronger than courtesy— he introduced himself, he begged her pardon for what he was going to do, and he began to inspect the recumbent body so as to see if his instructions had been followed. He stuck his index finger into her navel and confirmed that by pushing on it lightly and turning from left to right, as if it were a screw, the hollow of the navel became an opening through which it was possible to introduce a few gallons of hot water so that the body would lose the statuary rigidity of plastic and take on the natural heat of the human body with all of its nobilities and destitution and the mobility and consistency of any young, vital, adventure and pleasure-loving body.

At the pinnacle of happiness, Richardson hurried to heat the necessary water, he invited the baroness to come out of the box-coffin, gallantly offering his hand, he lay her down on his own bed and with a funnel made expressly for this operation, he proceeded to fill the hollow body as if he were feeding a fetus through an umbilical cord. Little by little, the body took on vitality, the face stretched in a seductive smile, she smiled with the satisfaction with which Adam must have smiled when his soul was blown upon and he felt himself alive. Richardson meticulously closed the screw top of the navel and, standing her up, he helped her walk to the bathroom, where he made her stand on the scale. The needle pointed to exactly the seventy kilograms of weight which corresponded to her height.

From that moment on, Richardson no longer had a statue in his apartment, nor a plastic doll: he had the baroness. The hot water had achieved its objective in such a way that her nakedness made him uncomfortable. He couldn't look at her when he spoke to her, so he buttoned up the three buttons on the blouse, he wrapped her hips in a towel, he sat her down on the living room sofa, he asked her permission to withdraw, and he ran out to buy her a complete trousseau, which was not difficult, since he knew her exact measurements and had studied her tastes and her favorite colors. In the shop, he chose clothing suitable for an exotic, sensual woman who was not exactly elegant, because in spite of being a baroness and everything, she was more inclined toward exuberance than toward refinement. He knew that she adored jewels and flowing drapery, the showy and the risqué and the colors that went with her dark skin. Her tastes did not accord with her aristocratic title and were, moreover, entirely the opposite of Richardson's. He would have chosen to dress her as the young women of his country dressed, or like the tourists who went to the islands, with casual shirts, blue jeans, and tennis shoes that were cheaper and more comfortable, but he preferred to comply with her tastes.

A few days later, managing to shake off the journalists

and photographers, linked closely arm in arm, they embarked for the islands. This time they didn't take any tour for bakers, but rather the tour for those honeymooning in the islands. On the plane, not even the flight attendants noticed that they were serving Coca-Cola and liqueurs to a plastic doll. She leaned her head on his shoulder, and since they had their fingers intertwined, the discreet cabin attendants tried to pass quickly by the seats occupied by the sugary couple.

As soon as the plane touched down, Richardson busied himself with the task of helping her to descend and when he touched the soil and smelled the salty air, he realized that the old one no longer interested him, because in reality, the one who interested him, with whom he was even in love, was the plastic body that he carried with him, very close to his side, very romantically indulged and desired more than she should have been because she began to be the only meaning in his life. The two identified with each other and they loved each other. Everything related to the flesh and blood one had lost its meaning, seeming so absurd and distant that he could not understand why he had filled up his luggage with so many books and magazines that talked about her. So that when they were settled in what would be their new home, he made up a package with *Satan Came to Eden* by Dora Strauch; with *Floreana, lista de correos*, by Margret Wittmer; with *The Last Enchanted Islands*, by Paulette Rendon; with *La isla de los gatos negros*, by Vásconez Hurtado; with *Floreana, paraíso infernal*, by

Maurice Brezieres and with every brochure, magazine, or clipping that he had saved and collected. He put the packet under the bed, secretly, pushing it with the tip of his toe, as if he were afraid that the new one would find out about the existence of the other, and because he loved her so much that he would not have wanted to provoke a jealous scene in their new home. With the new direction that his feelings were taking, he decided to stay and live in the islands forever. Everything else could go to the devil. He was in love like a schoolboy and thus he lived happily in an extended honeymoon that stretched well beyond the time it might be reasonable for a passionate romance to last. And when his money began to run out, threatening to destroy the idyll—because he wasn't going to treat her to hamburgers and Coca-Cola all the time, because this wasn't a *with you, bread and onions* kind of woman, she was champagne and caviar—he began to think about how to survive, until the lucky star that had always accompanied him came to his aid.

One day, he saw a plane land at an unusual hour. He deduced that this had something to do with him, since he was quite an important figure and, in effect, a motor launch unknown in the islands docked at the pier. The passengers who arrived on the launch also flew seated in the same so as not to waste time. As soon as the plane touched down, the launch was already cutting through the crystalline waters and within a few moments the travelers were in front of Richardson. They found him drinking lemonade with the baroness, seated in the shade of the rosy bougainvilleas and enjoying life. They talked for a long time and left close to nightfall.

A few days later, the surprised people of the islands saw the arrival of an enormous ship that anchored far from the pier, not so much due to its deep draft as out of a certain discretion that surrounded the landing of a gigantic cargo of boxes. The ship's sailors worked all night with the instinctive organization of ants and the next day, the inhabitants of the islands woke up to a faint, disquieting scent that filled the entire body with unforgettable memories and the entire mouth with saliva. The whole island smelled of bread, of freshly baked bread which made them leap out of bed and go en masse in search of the scent, and they saw that, as if by the most magical of magics, a new business had been installed, complete down to the smallest detail, missing nothing, not even the sign at the entrance.

When they arrived, they were left mute with surprise at seeing the miracle of a bakery so perfectly constructed and organized while they slept. It seemed to have risen from the misty drizzle of the early morning, from the whirlwinds of the pale sand, from the depths of the murmuring sea, from the most incredible technology competing with a chapter out of science fiction. They saw Richardson with a white apron and without the baroness at his side sliding in and pulling out from a brand new oven trays and more trays of a bread so golden and fresh that it seemed impossible that it could be made in the wild islands.

Richardson shared out his bread in abundance, and he did it for free because it was the grand opening of the Hot Cakes Bakery, which was written on a big sign that crowned the door to the business. And from then on, he sold hot bread twice a day and the inhabitants of the island began to gain weight like crazy. Nevertheless, nine months later, the incidental, detachable fatness of the women stopped happening; they got fat only due to gastronomical causes, not marital ones. From then on, not one child was born; the women dried up inside in the same way that Brigita's spring had dried up, and the numen of the poet Alirio, and the insides of Yerma.

Richardson lost interest in the baroness, he left her thoughtlessly exposed to the equatorial sun while the finches pecked at her nose and cheeks, filling her neglected wig and her clothing with their ridiculous excrement. Often, busy with his new work, he forgot to take her out to enjoy the cool of the evening. Days and days passed without him saying a word to her, or lying down with her, or changing her clothes, or giving her anything to eat or drink. The baroness cried out for a bath. The assiduous red ants climbed up her shapely legs single file and the black spiders, with their long, long legs that looked like little wire tables, wove their webs in her private parts. She was not even the shadow of her former self. Until one day, he forgot to change the water that she had had inside her for months, and the water went bad, ruining the dark skin of her body and her face and the slenderness and the firmness of her limbs. Lust became lack, sensuality became senility, desire became dirt and she fell off the chair on which she had been sitting for quite some time. Then Richardson understood that that's how life is... and that the best he could do under the circumstances was to give Christian burial to she who until then had been his lover.

He dug a hole in the burning sand—not very deep because the sun was scorching his back and it was the hour of the siesta. He quickly wrapped up the pitiful body that the worms would eat, using a white towel by way of a shroud, and he dragged her by the feet to the grave, and when he scattered the last shovelful of soil, he felt so awful that he vomited onto the tomb. He knew well that it was not due to the smell of rotten rubber, but rather because in the deepest part of his ancestral Puritanism, he felt criminal and dishonest. He was so overcome with grief that he felt embarrassed to bury her like a dog—after all, she had been his companion for a long time. Because of her he had come to the islands and they had spent unforgettable moments together.

He threw the shovel aside and went running to the house of San Pío Pascual and Santa Livina, and when he got there he begged them in his terrible, breathless Spanish to conduct some kind of religious ceremony over the recently dug grave. San Pío Pascual shook his head obstinately, looking on him (pityingly) as a profane blasphemer and crazy gringo who nevertheless made the best bread that he had ever eaten, and he turned his back on him with dignity.

Richardson threatened, more by signs than with words, that if he didn't do what he asked, he would stop baking bread and would go away forever, flying like an albatross, to his native land. Santa Livina jumped when she understood what he was saying and, taking San Pío Pascual by the arm, she whispered certain arguments and as always she persuaded him. Then, with an ill grace, he looked for his tools of salvation and he began to walk dejectedly, as if he were pushed by obligation or conscience. He arrived at the foot of the newly dug grave and said a prayer for the dead that had all the characteristics of a slap in the face. Richardson was satisfied. He prayed for a few moments with his head uncovered and without further ado, set out dragging his feet toward the bakery to prepare the four o'clock bread.

With the baroness dead and buried, which was the same as saying *the dead in their holes and the living eat rolls*, Richardson devoted himself with more frenzy than ever to his former trade of baker. The ship that had come, bringing the bakery in pieces, appeared as regularly as the full moon with its cargo of flour and other ingredients with which he kneaded, baked, and sold the best and cheapest bread of all the breads in the world, bread that disappeared as soon as it came out of the oven.

"True ees it exterordinary?" asked Richardson, excited and pleased with the kindness of his own country and with the proof of such high karat altruism toward the inhabitants of the islands. He settled the books and found that it was no business for anyone, save only he himself, who received a good salary and pocketed the proceeds for work that was almost a sport. He clearly did not understand it all, but that must be how the aid of a big country to a small country worked. He felt himself the intermediary of the purest, most quintessential philanthropy. It seemed to him that he was not standing in front of the kneading table, but standing in the middle of the Pacific Ocean, standing without sinking, as if he were the selfsame Statue of Liberty, but not with the arm holding the torch of liberty above his head, rather with his arms extended in a cross, pulling, with the strength of a colossus, from north to south, the arm of a power both admired and admirable, the powerful arm that waited serenely so that Richardson might pull from the south to the north the scrawny arm of an unknown country lost on the map so that both countries could, before his lean waist that emerged from the waters like a symbol, meet in a strong handshake, even if it were that of a huge mitt with a tiny little hand. And he felt for the same reason more noble in flesh and in spirit, more a providential protector, more paternally good, more effective than all the Peace Corps, redeemed for his prior lack of attention to the baroness, which had carried her to her grave. And he baked his bread with a passionate, apostolic frenzy, with the same enthusiasm and dedication with which long ago he had investigated the trail of she who had been his lover and now lay in a Christian grave.

The inhabitants of the islands adapted to the bread

from the very first day. The ovens never went out because the scent of bread spread to the other islands. There was such demand that once the Hot Cakes Bakery opened, the ships previously dedicated to the mail and to inter-island commerce, threw aside the satchels of correspondence and openly took up the transport of fragrant and inexpensive loaves, baguettes, and tasty little rolls. The people, eating and getting fat, resembled the cormorants more all the time. Satisfied and grateful, they rendered their tribute of love and gratitude to the foreigner.

But that day, when Richardson finished taking the first trays of the night's bread out of the oven, he was surprised to find that his usual clientele wasn't loitering around, swallowing in advance our daily bread. He went to the door and was more surprised still to see that the street was completely deserted in spite of it being a Sunday. There was no one, not one of all the people who came out of the church that had not yet been built—which was almost everyone in town—not one of those who were in the habit of anchoring at the bakery doors as if they were continuing the religious service.

There was a silence full of suspicions, without a soul around. Nor could Richardson suppose that no one had attended the religious ceremony officiated by San Pío Pascual and Santa Livina and that the church that had not yet been built had remained deserted, as if the people had all agreed that today didn't have to be Sunday, but could be any other day of the week, for which reason no one noticed that San Pío Pascual spilled the wine on the cloth of the improvised table which stood in for an altar or that Santa Livina forgot to ring the little bells that weren't really bells, but instead two little round stones placed in the belly of an old bronze chocolate pot.

Richardson planted himself in the middle of the deserted street and sadly asked the evening wind, "Whar ur they that not to smell the bread? What will happen that they not to came?"

But the wind kept to its impetuous course without answering him. He walked down to the beach in search of his clientele. There they were, men and women sitting on top of a tragic silence, surveying the shadows, overwhelmed with guilt. To one side, Brigita's remains were still smoking. Richardson took a long time to understand, barely guessing at the horrible crime. It was hard for him to pull his ingenuously blue eyes away from the red-hot coals; it seemed absurd to see what he was seeing and to reach the certainty that it was true.

Meanwhile, the men were dying of thirst before the nearby paradox of the immensity of the sea. And the water of the sea was completely useless for removing the soot from their hands, although they washed with the desperate tenacity of Lady Macbeth.

Far away, San Pío Pascual and Santa Livina, seated on the stones that served as stairs for the church that had not yet been built, looked at the cloud of smoke and felt themselves sprouting a rush as of flight that was pushing them out of the islands. But the sea with its liquid walls was an impassable barrier that backed them into the corner of sin. And when the true night came with its ancestral fears and it was the hour in which Estenia usually passed on the beach, the people saw the familiar, human firefly come flying. They breathed out with relief, thinking that someone in the great beyond remembered them, but suddenly, in the heat of the bonfire, Estenia suspended her flight and brusquely changed the course of her circuit, dousing her light with a shudder, and they never, never again saw her flying with her little spark of light over the dead sands of the beach.

Then the men began to feel desperate and the women started in with the useless weeping. When the tears and the desperation ran out, they saw the decrepit, black rat coming, the one that sprouted a pair of wrinkled wings to make itself a bat and frighten Iridia. The rat slipped, step by step, between the legs of the penitents who, full of revulsion and terror, did not even have the strength to shoo it away. The black rat, dragging its plague and its horror, walked down to the beach and by its own volition, drowned itself in the sea. The waves became higher as if to reject it and its remains were lost in the icy waters of Alaska.

Everyone understood that they had lost forever the power to glimpse the souls of things. They knew that they were cursed and that they could not live in the islands as before. Finally, Morgan appeared with the gloomy *tock-tock* of his wooden leg. Without giving a thought to his otherworldly appearance, he approached each one of them.

He began to whisper in their ears about the existence of the treasure and the possibility of digging it up and becoming rich. He broke their souls, which were already twisted. Their souls split in two and they were filled with greed. They began to look for the gold chain, digging in the soil as if in each pit they wished to bury themselves along with the bundle of their guilt. They dug day and night with the force of destruction without finding anything, because Morgan mocked them, giving them false leads. To bore through the earth and remove the big rocks, they divided into groups, and when they were divided, they began to recognize their enormous failure. They got even first by attacking with words, calling each other murderers for the death of Brigita, and then they attacked for real, leading to extermination.

Their sooty hands were further marked with homicidal blood. The bony one went around collecting the bodies, no longer one by one, as she had always done it, but in a long, single file that she dragged across the sand and that smelled bad. The spring remained dry, emphasizing their thirst and the reddish-black of their hands. Between the *orchilla* bushes, between the tall *Opuntias* and the black rocks, the two bands spied on each other, they hunted and exterminated each other. Right on the surface, they bore the regressive instincts of a war without quarter in which Morgan never stopped urging them on. The gusts of wind brought the echo of his harsh, loud laughter. The iguanas slithered over the basalt, hiding the fear they began to feel in their dorsal spines. The finches stopped pecking at the food on people's plates. The cormorants walked on the beach dragging their degenerated wings and suffering for having lost their capacity to fly. The tortoises hid their wrinkled heads under their centuries-old shells because the air of the islands had an unhealthy smell.

All of them were extinguished, but San Pío Pascual and Santa Livina were left to tell the tale after their fashion, and the news traveled to the mainland:

MYSTERIOUS PLAGUE ATTACKS ISLAND SETTLERS, DECIMATING POPULATION.

Alone, left to themselves, without parishioners and without friends, they left the islands. They went sadly, downcast with the sorrow of not having been able to build the church and with the weight of Brigita's death. They embarked on the first ship that arrived to see what had happened, and only when they were far out at sea did the islands feel the call of terra firma, they turned around as if they wanted to shake off human misery and its wasting passions and they settled definitively in the same place as before. Villamil's cables, with which they were tied, knotted themselves again and then remained fixed forever. The iguanas went back to slithering tranquilly, spitting out every trace of fear; the tortoises once again incubated time under their mobile bunkers; the birds returned to their peaceful flights and to pecking at the same plate from which people ate.

Meanwhile, Richardson confirmed his suspicion that he had been used. He understood why Iridia had always detested him, why Estenia tried to pierce his brain with the inquisition of her gaze. He knew that the loaves that left his diligent hands, rose on his table like little bellies, and toasted in his ovens that were never turned off, were all equally criminal: they contained a high dose of contraceptives mixed in with the flour brought by the big ship.

One morning, when all of the dead were buried and there were hardly any living to eat the bread from the Hot Cakes Bakery, he surprised the bony one who was spying on him from between the sacks of flour. He was saddened, because he was far from his homeland and did not want to die among strangers, but he gathered his courage and taking the tools with which in days gone by he had dug the grave of his companion, he destroyed the entire building, and when it was razed to the ground, leaving only a river of flour, he went to weep for his naivety over the remains of his rotted baroness. Then the pallid one touched him. His tears ended. He went to the shore with his shirt open and his chest to the wind as if he wanted the bony one to touch him again. The bony one returned, full of lust; she put her hand on Richardson's chest, but he did not fall. He remained standing while the wind gathered all the flour and covered him. Then he felt a soft blow as his own head hit his shoulders, his cervical vertebrae sank into his sternum, and when he wanted to confirm that he no longer had a neck, he realized that he had lost his hands, arms, and forearms. He tried to walk and found that he had no feet, nor legs, nor knees and he was entirely naked and covered with flour. He had no eyes, nor mouth, nor nose; he was like a gigantic loaf in the shape of a penis that sought to get itself into all the women with a disproportionate haste so as to conceive the children that they had wanted but been unable to have.

Richardson wanted to be the creative force, but it was too late; he wanted to be the sower and not the man sated with lust, the greenhouse and not the brutal macho, the father of those who would be born and repopulate the islands and not the bellowing stud that frightened the women. Later, when he tried to keep himself upright, he fell on his side and felt how the finches came in flocks to peck at him. As he had no hands, he couldn't shoo them away. As he had no feet, he could not escape and when the people saw the flock of birds they went to see what was happening and they found an immense loaf lying on the beach. It didn't matter what shape it had, it was bread and they were hungry. They tore off big hunks. It didn't have the same flavor as the bread from the Hot Cakes Bakery, but it was bread.

Richardson felt them remove a piece of leg and he didn't feel pain; they tore off a piece of arm and he shuddered at feeling himself placed between the people's teeth. He felt them tear off a piece of belly and part of his back and he didn't mind passing through the dark, humid esophagus.

He felt them take away a piece of his head and he saw himself trapped by the gastric juices of the stomach where the action of the contraceptives that the women had taken was neutralized. Only then did Richardson feel something like pain, as he sank into a nothingness that was like a dark bridge toward the infinite.

When the new generation was formed by the bolus that was Richardson who kept going through the maternal caverns to insinuate himself into the fallopian tubes and do his cleansing work in the ovaries, a new colony of people appeared who seemed strange but were not. They knew the real value of time and for that reason had no hurry. They didn't feel the urgency to have things, because the miasmas of the most decadent civilization that the old world saw be born, grow up, and die, were far away from them. The men learned a new way of living, respecting the rights of those who had priority in the islands. They asked permission of the fauna and the flora to sit down beside them and contemplate the sunsets and the dawns, and to be able to look inside themselves, seeking to transcend and understanding the reasons of the souls of things.

The accusations of yesteryear were no longer heard. The Germans no longer said of the settlers, "those lazybones that don't know how to work," nor did the colonists say of the Germans, "those animals that kill themselves working."

The bony one declared herself in the most unusual of rebellions: she stopped appearing to the people she was going to carry off. She no longer took the faded and terrifying form of a skeleton wrapped in black rags. She would appear from time to time as a modern girl, in blue jeans and t-shirt, and she wore her hair gathered in a long and silky ponytail. She went into the houses and shops. She bathed in the sea in a miniscule bikini. She had boyfriends. She was the friend and confidant of the women and even the baby-sitter for the infants.

In the islands there was space for those who wanted to flee from devastating civilization and there was a place for those born at the margins of the same. The whole universe fit in that place. The spring reappeared on common property. The new inhabitants of the islands had Morgan's vitality, they were happy and mixed, they could live off poetry like Alirio, they were able to give themselves to their neighbors like Iridia, they had in their hands Prometheus' torch like Estenia, they were lovers of the bare-breasted woman like Fritz, they fled from sorrow like Tarsilia, they had the gift of curing illness like Brigita, and they knew that they were truly in paradise.

About the Author

ALICIA YÁNEZ COSSÍO was born in 1928 in Quito, Ecuador, where she still resides. Educated in Ecuador and in Spain. She was awarded a Medal of Cultural Achievement of the First Class by the national government in 1990 and is a member of the Ecuadorian Academy of the Spanish Language. In 2008, she was awarded Ecuador's Premio Eugenio Espejo, the most prestigious national prize offered in the arts and humanities.

About the Translator

AMALIA GLADHART first learned Spanish while living in Mira, in northern Ecuador. Educated at Michigan State and at Cornell University, she is Associate Professor of Spanish at the University of Oregon. Her translation of Alicia Yánez Cossío's *The Potbellied Virgin* was published in 2006. Her poetry and short fiction have appeared in the Iowa Review, Bellingham Review, Seneca Review, Stone Canoe, and elsewhere.

Also Available from **UNOPRESS** :

William Christenberry: Art & Family by J. Richard Gruber (2000)

The El Cholo Feeling Passes by Fredrick Barton (2003)

A House Divided by Fredrick Barton (2003)

Coming Out the Door for the Ninth Ward edited by Rachel Breunlin
from The Neighborhood Story Project series (2006)

The Change Cycle Handbook by Will Lannes (2008)

*Cornerstones: Celebrating the Everyday Monuments & Gathering
Places of New Orleans* edited by Rachel Breunlin,
from The Neighborhood Story Project series (2008)

A Gallery of Ghosts by John Gery (2008)

Hearing Your Story: Songs of History and Life for Sand Roses by Nabile
Farès translated by Peter Thompson,
from The Engaged Writers Series (2008)

The Imagist Poem: Modern Poetry in Miniature edited by William Pratt
from The Ezra Pound Center for Literature series (2008)

The Katrina Papers: A Journal of Trauma and Recovery
by Jerry W. Ward, Jr. from The Engaged Writers Series (2008)

On Higher Ground: The University of New Orleans at Fifty
by Dr. Robert Dupont (2008)

Us Four Plus Four: Eight Russian Poets Conversing
translated by Don Mager (2008)

Voices Rising: Stories from the Katrina Narrative Project
edited by Rebeca Antoine (2008)

Gravestones (Lápidas) by Antonio Gamoneda,
translated by Donald Wellman from The Engaged Writers Series (2009)

The House of Dance and Feathers: A Museum by Ronald W. Lewis by
Rachel Breunlin & Ronald W. Lewis,
from The Neighborhood Story Project series (2009)

I hope it's not over, and good-by: Selected Poems of Everette Maddox
by Everette Maddox (2009)

Portraits: Photographs in New Orleans 1998-2009
by Jonathan Traviesa (2009)

Theoretical Killings: Essays & Accidents by Steven Church (2009)

Voices Rising II: More Stories from the Katrina Narrative Project
edited by Rebeca Antoine (2010)

Rowing to Sweden: Essays on Faith, Love, Politics, and Movies
by Fredrick Barton (2010)

Dogs in My Life: The New Orleans Photographs
of John Tibule Mendes (2010)

Understanding the Music Business: A Comprehensive View
edited by Harmon Greenblatt & Irwin Steinberg (2010)
The Fox's Window by Naoko Awa, translated by Toshiya Kamei (2010)
A Passenger from the West by Nabile Farès,
translated by Peter Thompson from The Engaged Writers Series (2010)
The Schüssel Era in Austria: Contemporary Austrian Studies, Volume 18
edited by Günter Bischof & Fritz Plasser (2010)
The Gravedigger by Rob Magnuson Smith (2010)
Everybody Knows What Time It Is by Reginald Martin (2010)
When the Water Came: Evacuees of Hurricane Katrina by Cynthia Hogue
& Rebecca Ross from The Engaged Writers Series (2010)
Aunt Alice Vs. Bob Marley by Kareem Kennedy,
from The Neighborhood Story Project series (2010)
Houses of Beauty: From Englishtown to the Seventh Ward
by Susan Henry from The Neighborhood Story Project series (2010)
Signed, The President by Kenneth Phillips,
from The Neighborhood Story Project series (2010)
Beyond the Bricks by Daron Crawford & Pernell Russell
from The Neighborhood Story Project series (2010)
Green Fields: Crime, Punishment, & a Boyhood Between by Bob Cowser,
Jr., from the Engaged Writers Series (2010)
New Orleans: The Underground Guide by Michael Patrick Welch
& Alison Fensterstock (2010)
Writer in Residence: Memoir of a Literary Translater
by Mark Spitzer (2010)
Open Correspondence: An Epistolary Dialogue by Abdelkébir Khatibi
and Rita El Khayat, translated by Safoi Babana-Hampton, Valérie K.
Orlando, Mary Vogl from The Engaged Writers Series (2010)
Black Santa by Jamie Bernstein (2010)
*From Empire to Republic: Post-World-War-I Austria: Contemporary
Austrian Studies*, Volume 19 edited by Günter Bischof, Fritz Plasser and
Peter Berger (2010)
Vegetal Sex (O Sexo Vegetal) by Sergio Medeiros,
translated by Raymond L.Bianchi (2010)
Dream-Crowned (Traumgekrönt) by Rainer Maria Rilke,
translated by Lorne Mook (2010)
Wounded Days (Los Días Heridos) by Leticia Luna,
translated by Toshiya Kamei from The Engaged Writers Series (2010)